# BEASTS OF OLYMPUS

## HOUND OF HADES

Lucy Coats is the author of more than thirty books for readers of all ages, including *Atticus the Storyteller's 100 Greek Myths*, which was shortlisted for the Blue Peter Book Award. She began her storytelling career as a bookseller, editor and journalist, and has been fascinated by myths and legends ever since she can remember. She lives in deepest south Northamptonshire with her husband and three unruly dogs. When she is not writing, she cooks, grows vegetables and sits in her stone circle, looking at the stars.

# BEASTS OF OLYMPUS

## HOUND OF HADES

### LUCY COATS

with illustrations by
David Roberts

Piccadilly
PRESS

First published in Great Britain in 2015
by Piccadilly Press
Northburgh House, 10 Northburgh Street, London EC1V 0AT
www.piccadillypress.co.uk

A CIP catalogue record for this book is available
from the British Library.

ISBN: 978–1–84812–440–0

1 3 5 7 9 10 8 6 4 2

Typeset in Bembo by Palimpsest Book Production Limited,
Falkirk, Stirlingshire

Printed in the UK by Clays Ltd, St Ives plc

Piccadilly Press is an imprint of the Bonnier Publishing Group
www.bonnierpublishing.com

For Samuel and Matteo
from their Great Aren'ty

# 1

# OFFICIAL BEASTKEEPER TO THE GODS

Demon, brand-new Official Beastkeeper to the Gods and son of Pan, god of the forests, had a bellyache.

It was a bellyache of monumental proportions. Even Atlas the Titan had never had a bellyache as big as this one, Demon decided.

He lay under his blanket in the loft above the stables and wished he hadn't eaten those final ten honey cakes the goddess Hestia had pressed on him as a 'going home snack'. He was still so full after the gods' feast last night to celebrate his new position that he hadn't slept a wink. The prospect of his usual early morning task of shovelling barrows full of poo down to the hundred-armed monsters in Tartarus was making him feel greener than mouldy spinach. He groaned and turned over on his straw mattress, closing his eyes and wishing that Eos, goddess of the dawn, would hold off on opening up the day. She always insisted on flinging back her pink sunrise curtains so horribly early. Couldn't she just give everyone a lie-in for once?

'Oi! Demon! I'm hungry! Where's my breakfast?' came a loud shout from below. There was a scrape and clatter of claws on the ladder, then Arnie the griffin popped its head through the trapdoor, leaned over and poked its sharp beak into Demon's aching stomach.

'Go 'way, Arnie,' Demon moaned. 'I'm ill. Very ill. In fact, I may die any minute now.'

'Huh!' said Arnie. 'Well, I wouldn't lie around dying for too long. I hear from the nymphs that you're going to have an Important Visitor this morning. One who won't be too impressed with a lazy stable boy who HASN'T FED HIS CHARGES!' As Arnie yelled the last four words, he snatched Demon's blanket away and nipped at his bare toes till they bled.

'Ouch! All RIGHT! I'm coming.' Demon leapt out of bed and threw on his chiton, muttering crossly as Offy and Yukus, the two healing snakes who lived in the magical collar he'd been given by Hephaestus, the blacksmith god, set to work mending his poor bloody toes. Compared to some of the dreadful wounds Demon had suffered when he first started in the Stables of the Gods it was an easy job and they were soon done. It was just a pity they didn't deal with sore tummies as well.

'What important visitor?' he asked, when Offy and Yukus had slithered back up around his neck and he'd finally managed to belt his silver rope around his waist at the fourth attempt.

'Aha!' said Arnie mysteriously, tapping one grubby claw against its beak.

'You are a very annoysome creature sometimes,' said Demon. 'Anyway, I don't have time to worry about some stupid visitor. As you so kindly reminded me just now, I've got work to do.'

But as he descended the ladder a small nervous

lump lodged itself somewhere just above his solar plexus. What if the important visitor was Hera? What if she had another impossible task for him to do like getting all nine heads back on Doris the Hydra? He'd only just managed that. What if she threatened to turn him into a little heap of charcoal again? He could hear Arnie giggling above him. That was never usually good news.

By the time he'd mucked out the Cattle of the Sun and fed them their special belly-gas busting golden hay, tipped leftover ambrosia cake into all the other immortal creatures' mangers, including the ever-hungry Arnie, and made sure the nymphs had milked the unicorns, Demon had a pounding headache and his stomach felt like a herd of man-eating horses were galloping about in it. Luckily his new friend the nine-headed Hydra had helped him out, carrying buckets, rakes, mops and brooms for him in all its mouths and pushing the poo-barrow with its tail.

'Thanks, Doris,' he said as he tipped the last of the stinky mess down the poo chute to the appreciative roars of the hundred-armed monsters who lived below. Doris grinned at him, its hundreds of sharp teeth glinting in the pale sunlight reflecting off Eos's pink fluffy bedsheets, which were hanging out to dry in the dawn sky. It loved having a proper name, and was so grateful to Demon for saving its life that it would do almost anything for him.

'Doris likes helping,' it said. Then it fluttered its twenty-seven pairs of long green eyelashes at Demon. 'Snackics for Doris now?' it asked hopefully.

Demon tossed it a few bits of leftover ambrosia cake and Doris retired to a corner of the stables to chew them. There was soon a spreading pool of drool beneath it – the Hydra was a messy eater at the best of times. With his work done, Demon headed over to the hospital shed – maybe Hephaestus's magical medicine box would have something to make his stomach feel better. He was meant to use the box for the beasts, really, but at this point he didn't care. He just wanted to feel normal again. As he opened the door to the shed, the comforting smell of aloe- and lavender-soaked bandages wafted out to greet him. The place was as neat as a pin – all the instruments gleaming and clean as they hung on the white painted walls. The big square silver box lay on the table in front of him.

As he lifted the lid, the familiar soft blue symbols sprang to life.

'State the nature of your beast's emergency medical problem,' the box said in its metallic voice.

'It's not a beast. It's me,' said Demon, rubbing his poor stomach and feeling very sorry for himself all over again. 'I've got a horrible bellyache and a thumping headache and I think I might die if you don't do something about it.' He didn't mention that the bellyache was from eating too many of Hestia's honey cakes. The box could be temperamental at times.

A long silver tentacle with a flat disc on the end of it shot out of the box and snaked down the front of Demon's chiton, making him jump. It was cold. After a few seconds it retreated back the way it had come.

'Error code 435. Human ailment. Does not compute with data program. Unable to assist. Thank you for your enquiry.' The box closed abruptly, with a final-sounding click.

'Stupid box,' said Demon, kicking the table so the box rattled. It opened a fraction to reveal a pointed silver tongue sticking out in Demon's direction, made a very rude farting noise, and snapped shut again immediately.

As he stalked crossly out of the hospital shed, slamming the door behind him, Demon saw a swirling clot of utter darkness burst out of a large crack in the ground. It was quite close by, and he was sure it hadn't been there five minutes before. It came racing towards him at an alarming speed, making a sound like a thousand pounding hammers. His heart began to thump, and a million butterflies started to flutter in his chest, joining the trampling horses in his stomach. This must be Arnie's Important Visitor arriving. Demon began to run towards the stables through the faint cloud of sadness that now hung in the air.

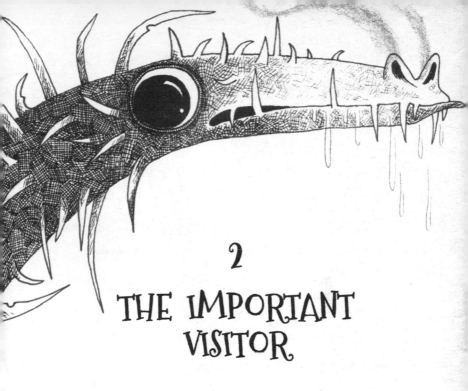

# 2
# THE IMPORTANT VISITOR

Demon reached the double doors of the stables just before the thundering clot of darkness did. He straightened his chiton hurriedly and ran his fingers through his curly hair, hoping there wasn't any straw in it. As a large, pointy-booted foot emerged from the inky murk, Demon caught a whiff of something strange — sort of damp and fusty-musty, a smell of old, dead things mixed in with the scent of burning hair. The foot was followed by a tall figure, cloaked all in black. On its head was a huge helmet, studded with blood-red rubies, and in its gloved right hand it held a set of reins, which it tossed to Demon. The reins appeared to be attached to something (or some *things*) within the blackness.

'Hurry up and ssstable those for me, dear boy,' the figure said, its sibilant voice soft and dangerous. 'And find them sssome meat, will you? That useless ssatyr Sssilenus tried to feed them leftover ambrosssia cake last time I was here. They burned all the hair off his legsss, if I recall correctly.' With that, the figure strode off towards Zeus and Hera's palace, leaving Demon staring open-mouthed after it.

'He arrived then, I see,' said Arnie into his left ear, nearly making Demon drop the reins.

'Who . . . what . . . ?' he stammered. 'Er, I mean . . . who IS that?' Demon asked, finally managing to get his words out properly.

'That? Oh, that's Hades. Lord of the Underworld. Terror of Tartarus. God of Death,' said Arnie. 'Bit overwhelming, isn't he?' It sniffed. 'I see he's brought those wretched things with him again,' it remarked sourly. 'His pride and joy, they are, but I wish he'd stick to horses. Better put them in the fireproof pens at the end, stable boy – they nearly torched the place when they were here before. And as for what they did to poor old Silenus . . . it doesn't bear thinking about. He had blisters for months.'

Demon gave an experimental tug on the reins Hades had so casually thrown him. They seemed to be made of some kind of pliable blue-black metal, light but very strong. Whatever was at the other end roared and tugged back, and two huge jets of blue-white flame lanced out of the darkness straight at him. Demon and Arnie ducked and rolled out of the way just in time, as five bales of the Cattle of the Sun's special hay frizzled into nothingness behind them.

'Play them your dad's pipes, quick!' yelled Arnie, through the sound of yet more roaring and spurts of fire. 'Don't know if they work on earth dragons, but it's worth a try!' Then it disappeared round the corner of the stables.

Demon hung on to the lashing, thrashing reins with one hand while fumbling in the pocket of his

chiton with the other. Dragons? he thought. *Dragons?*
DRAGONS! His legs wanted to run and his
frantically beating heart felt like it might easily escape
from his chest. He'd met and survived some terrifying
beasts already, but dragons were in a whole other
league.

Demon wrenched Pan's magic silver pipes out of
his pocket, swung them to his lips with one swift
movement and started to play. The cascade of tinkling
notes dropped into the roaring flames, and immediately
the reins fell limp and quiet in Demon's other hand.
A sort of crooning noise came from the darkness, and
then first one and then another great scaly bronze head
emerged out of the gloom. Their huge eyes were as
big as Hera's best golden dinner plates and deep purple
fires burned in their depths as they walked forward,
their enormous taloned feet making the ground shake
at every step. Sharp spikes and knobbly bits covered
their bodies in unassailable armour, and drifts of pale
smoke hung from their nostrils like ghosts of a fire.

Demon blew the pipes for all he was worth, not
daring to stop as he tugged the vast beasts towards
the rock-cave pens that lay at the very back of the

stables. He'd always wondered what creatures they were for. Now he knew.

If he'd thought getting the massive beasts into their pens was hard work, Demon soon found out that unharnessing sleepy earth dragons with one hand was almost impossible. He managed it eventually, using their armoured spikes as a ladder to reach the high bits, then throwing the undone metal straps outside the dragon pens for cleaning and polishing. He somehow knew without being told that Hades would expect them to be gleaming like fire opals when he returned. When he had finished, he walked out backwards, still playing the pipes, slammed the fireproof gates behind him and ran to a safe distance before he plucked up the courage to stop.

There was a sudden blissful silence. Not a beast in the stables was moving or making a noise. When he peeked into Arnie's cage, he saw the griffin was asleep on the floor, whiffling gently through its beak. All his other charges were the same – even the giant scorpion was lying on its back with its sting curled up. Demon grinned, looking at his trusty pipes.

'Thanks, Dad,' he whispered. His bellyache had

gone now and his head felt clear. He'd survived. Again. But then he remembered the other thing Hades had asked him to do. 'Meat. Where in the name of Zeus's toenails do I find meat?' he wondered. All there was to eat on Olympus usually was ambrosia cake. Except on feast days. Feast days . . . That was it! Maybe there was some meat left over from last night's feast. He definitely remembered seeing some roasted lamb legs going past on Hephaestus's magical serving trolleys. Demon shoved his pipes into his pocket again and set out for the forge under the mountain. The smith god always gave him good advice.

Hephaestus was lying down on a rocky couch, with a grimy blanket draped over him and a stained spotty handkerchief spread over his face. One of his silvery-gold robot automatons was pumping the forge bellows gently, keeping the fire to a muted glow. It raised a metal finger to its lips.

'Shh!' it said. Hephaestus's robots never used two words where one short one would do.

Demon looked at the god of the forge. Was it worth the risk of waking him? He wasn't the sort to turn a boy into charcoal – at least he hadn't been till now. But you never knew with the gods – they could turn nasty at any moment. Still, given the choice between Hades and Hephaestus being angry with him, he'd take his chances with Heffy any day. He drew in a deep breath and tiptoed over to the couch, ignoring the robot's attempts to keep him away.

He coughed quietly, then, as there was no response from the sleeping god, a little louder. Still nothing. One of Hephaestus's grubby, charcoal-dusted fingers poked out from under the blanket, so Demon bent down and tugged at it gently.

'Ahem! Hephaestus! Sir! Your Godishness! I wouldn't usually wake you, only it's a bit of an emergency . . .'

There was a snortling and a harrumphing from under the handkerchief, and thrown in between Demon caught a few indistinguishable words.

'Wassermatter? . . . snortle . . . thought Isaidnovisitors . . . harrumph . . . owmyheadhurts!'

Demon looked at the groaning god sympathetically. He knew exactly how Heffy felt. He bent down to try to rouse him again but just then

Hephaestus sat up unexpectedly, beard wild and snarly, eyes red-rimmed and half shut. The god's head met Demon's with a clash, knocking the boy backwards and into the robot, who fell over with a metallic crashing sound.

'AARRRGGHH!' roared the blacksmith god, leaping up and dancing about the forge, head in his enormous hands.

'OOOFF!' yelled Demon, as little bright stars of pain flared round his forehead and a heavy metal foot clipped his shoulder.

'I THOUGHT I GAVE ORDERS THAT I WAS NOT TO BE AWAKENED!' Hephaestus shouted, sparks flying from his eyes and the tips of his fingers. The robot said nothing. It was too busy collecting the pieces of itself and reattaching them.

'I'm v- v-very very sorry, it was all m-m-my fault,' said Demon in a small, quavery voice. He'd never seen Hephaestus this angry before, and he didn't want to again. The god was batting at his beard, which was now on fire from the sparks that had landed in it.

'Zeus-blasted stable boy,' said Hephaestus in slightly milder tones. 'What's so Hades-be-bothered important that you have to wake a god from his richly deserved beauty sleep?'

'Well,' said Demon, 'since you mention Hades . . .' He explained about the earth dragons needing meat, not ambrosia cake. 'I don't want to get my legs burnt off like poor Silenus did,' he finished. 'I don't think even Offy and Yukus could mend that.'

Hephaestus stood there for a moment, pulling clumps of singed beard out and scratching his head while he thought.

'Hestia,' he said finally. 'She usually supervises the clean-up after a feast. If there's any meat about she'll know where it's kept. Go and find her. She'll be in the kitchens.' He looked around him. 'Where's that wretched robot when you need it?' The robot stepped out from behind a pillar. 'Here, you – take Demon to the kitchens. He'll never find them otherwise. And put that arm on the right way round before you come back.' He limped over to his couch and lay down again, sighing loudly. 'Now go away and leave me to my headache.'

# 3

# THE KITCHENS OF
# THE GODS

The robot led Demon through the winding back alleyways of Olympus, past places he'd never seen before. He'd been so busy with the beasts since Pan had snatched him away from his village in Arcadia that there had been no time to explore properly. He hadn't realised that palaces had back doors with rubbish outside them, nor that the gods and goddesses would need normal things like washing lines. It all reminded him of home a bit too much, and suddenly his nose prickled fiercely as he remembered his mum hanging out their laundry. She'd only have one lot to do now.

Swallowing, and scrubbing one hand across his watery eyes, he ducked under a row of yellow spidersilk robes hung out to dry in the morning breeze. They smelled like soft sunshine and sweet flower petals as he brushed against them. Demon wanted to stop and look around, but the robot was setting a good pace with its long metal legs and he had to trot to keep up. Besides, he knew he had to find the meat for the earth dragons before Hades came back. He had a bad feeling that Hades might turn out to be almost as scary as Hera, but in a slithery kind of way.

As they turned into a white marble courtyard, a delicious aroma filled his nose. It was both familiar and unfamiliar at the same time. 'Mmm,' he said, sniffing with his eyes half closed. What was that? It smelled good. Suddenly his stomach rumbled loudly. He didn't know how he could be hungry again after last night's feast, but it appeared his stomach had different ideas.

'Kitchens,' said the robot, pointing with its good arm towards an open wooden door. Demon thanked it, and it turned without another word and took off at a run, wrenching its bad arm round to the right position as it went, making a metallic sort of tearing noise. Demon shuddered. It was a horrid sound. He went up to the door and put his head round it, peering in. Inside was a pantry with dirty gold and silver dishes on every surface. Hundreds of them. Almost as many jewelled goblets were piled up in heaps on the floor.

There seemed to be nobody about, so Demon went further in, picking his way round the chaos and through a second door to the right. He saw a huge kitchen, bustling with activity. This was where the delicious smell was coming from. There were small cooking fires burning everywhere, their flames reflected off the gleaming sides of a thousand copper pots, jugs and whole racks full of shining silver knives. Round the sides of the kitchen stood a series of long tables where nymphs were chopping and pouring and mixing. The air was full of the sound of sizzling, and in the middle of it all stood the goddess Hestia, a large wooden spoon in her hand, directing the whole operation. She had on the apron embroidered with pots and pans he'd last seen her wearing when he visited her palace to get some eternal flame to cure the Cretan Bull's bovine pentagastric marine pyrosaturitis. Its five fire-making stomachs had got waterlogged when horrible Heracles stabbed it in the heart. Close by her, several fauns, wearing smaller aprons, were working hard frying large quantities of some sort of long brown cylinder with rounded ends in enormous pans. Others were scurrying about, pulling trays of steaming bread out of huge ovens. One very small faun was standing on a stool beside Hestia, fanning her face with a large palm leaf. It was very very hot.

'Ah! Our Official Beastkeeper has arrived,' said Hestia. 'Hello, Pandemonius. Would you like one of my special loukaniko sausages for breakfast? They're a brand-new recipe – I added cinnamon and apples to the mix. All the gods and goddesses always want a cooked breakfast instead of ambrosia when they wake up after drinking Dionysus's silly grape juice.' As she spoke, she whipped a sausage out of the nearest pan, slapped it inside a hot bread roll and handed it to Demon. The smell was . . . well . . . divine. He bit into it, not caring that it was piping hot. It tasted utterly delicious, sweet and spicy and full of just the right amount of meat. Oh no! Meat. He'd forgotten his errand for a second.

'Yum!' he said hastily and indistinctly, chewing frantically. 'Yum, yum, YUM!' He didn't want to hurry this – it would be back to horrid ambrosia cake soon – but he knew he had to. 'Er, Your Goddessness, I was wondering . . .'

Hestia shoved another full roll into his free hand.

'Try this one,' she said. 'It's got pine nuts and just a touch of wild thyme honey – oh, and don't worry, I know what you've come for. I saw Hades come blowing past like a dreary deluge about half an hour ago. I expect he was cross at not being able to come to the feast last night. Glaukos over there is already loading up some supplies for those wretched dragons of his.' She pointed to a faun throwing what looked like large hunks of cooked flesh into a battered silver barrow. Demon felt like falling to his knees with gratitude. Hestia was definitely the nicest goddess ever.

'Fank you,' he mumbled, still chewing a mouthful of bread and sausage. Hestia just waved him towards the barrow, turning to whack a nearby faun round the horns with her wooden spoon. There was black smoke coming out of the frying pan he was looking after.

'Use those tongs!' she yelled. 'Did I say I wanted the sausages burnt to a crisp? I'll burn you to a crisp if you don't CONCENTRATE!'

Demon hurried away. Hestia might be nice, but he wasn't taking any risks.

All the beasts were still asleep when Demon got back to the stables, panting slightly from the exertion of pushing the heavy barrow full of meat. He tiptoed up to the rock-cave pens and unlocked the fireproof doors gingerly, pipes at the ready just in case. But both earth dragons were still slumped on the floor, small streams of ghostly smoke rising from two sets of cavern-like nostrils as they snored. He carted the meat in as quickly as he could and tossed it into the large stone trough gouged out of the wall, hoping they wouldn't wake up till he was out of there. He didn't fancy being in the same place as two hungry dragons. They might see him as a tasty snack to whet their appetite. Sure enough, just as he was fastening the doors there was a flash of flame, a great roaring and then loud chomping noises. Like most beasts, dragons obviously woke up at the smell of food.

Demon felt a sharp claw dig into his shoulder. 'Saved me some meat, did you, Pan's scrawny kid?' asked Arnie, menacingly. 'You'd better have.' Clearly the dragons were not the only ones to have been woken up by the smell of food. Luckily there were a couple of small legs of lamb left. Demon tossed them to the beast, who caught them in his huge curved beak.

'Eat them quietly,' he hissed at the creature. 'Or they'll all be wanting some.' Most of the beasts survived on stale ambrosia cake, but the more carnivorous ones complained about it dreadfully. Demon picked up the dragon harness and slung it over his shoulder with an effort. Although his muscles had got stronger from the effect of eating magical ambrosia cake – and also from all the shovelling and brushing and barrowing of poo he had to do on a daily basis – the mess of metal straps and breastplates was still very heavy. He hauled them out to the front of the stables and sat down on a bale of golden hay. What did you clean dragon harnesses with? he wondered.

The reins weren't too bad, but the bits were crusted with charcoaly spit from their mouths and the breastplates were disgusting, coated in icky things he didn't want to think too much about.

'Oh, Mel-anie,' he called. Melanie was a water naiad, the keeper of the spring outside the stables. He reckoned she would know about getting things clean. A blue head popped out of the water.

'What?' Melanie asked crossly. 'If the shampoo I lent you made your hair go green, it's not my fault.' Demon squinted upwards trying to see his hair. Nope. Still its usual mop of brown curls. He explained about the dragon harness. Melanie sighed.

'Don't you know anything, stable boy? Just ask the cleaning cupboard for what you need. It's in the second alcove to the right.' Then she disappeared with a splash that soaked the front of Demon's chiton. Sure enough, in the second alcove to the right was a small door that he'd never noticed before, marked with a tiny golden mop and bucket. Demon cleared his throat and tapped on it gently.

'I need something to clean Hades' earth dragons' harnesses with, please,' he said. The door sprang open and a metal arm shot out, nearly hitting him in the face. Clutched in its hand was a bottle marked 'Eternal All-Shine' and a large white cloth. Demon reached out and took them, wondering if this was yet another one of Heffy's marvellous inventions.

'Two drops should do the job,' said a high, fluting voice from within the cupboard. 'Please return all materials when finished.' Then the door snapped shut again. Twenty minutes later the harness was shining as if it was newly-made. Demon did as the cleaning cupboard had asked and put the bottle and cloth back, then hung the harness up neatly by the straps, ready for Hades' return. He just hoped he'd done a good enough job not to be roasted.

It turned out that he didn't have long to wait for the god of death. Just as he'd finished clearing away the clean white bones that were all Arnie had left of its meal, the bars of sunlight falling across the floor of the stables faded and turned to grey. There was a sudden breath of must and mould in the darkening air. Before Demon could even turn round, a heavy hand fell on his shoulder.

'Ssso, ssstable boy,' said Hades in his soft, hissing

voice. 'I sssee you haven't been eaten by my dragonsss. Yet.' There was a sinister pause, and then he went on, his fingers digging in so that Demon could feel the prick of his long nails. 'My sssister Hera tellsss me you're good with mending sssick beastsss. Are you?'

Demon didn't quite know what to say. If he said yes, it might sound like boasting. He knew the gods didn't like pride or boasting, especially the goddess Nemesis. A tiny finger of cold stroked down his spine as he remembered Narcissus, the proud boy who'd died staring at his own reflection. Nemesis was a lot more imaginative with her punishments than the gods who just burned humans into little piles of ash and soot.

'Well, Your M-m-mighty D-d-dark Godishness, I wouldn't say *good*, exactly. I've had a lot of help from my father and Hephaestus . . . a-and a bit of good fortune with my cures.' Demon kept his eyes fixed firmly on the floor, hoping that Hades would just go away and leave him alone now that he'd answered. But no such luck. The god clapped him on the shoulder so hard that Demon fell to his knees.

'A modessst boy. I like that. You'll need to pack up

your medical thingsss, ssstable boy. I need you in the Underworld for a while. I have a very poorly hound who needsss your attention urgently. Now, take me to my dragonsss. I have sssome treatsss for them.'

As Demon led Hades towards the dragon pens, his mind was whirling. The Underworld? Surely that was just for dead people – ghosts and shades? And what about the beasts he was supposed to take care of here on Olympus? Who would look after the stables if he was gone? He left Hades crooning to his dragons as if they were puppies and tossing strings of entrails in the air for them to catch. Then he took to his heels and ran as fast as he could to the hospital shed. As soon as he was inside, he scooped up some aloe and lavender bandages, which he stuffed inside his chiton, and grabbed his magical silver medicine box by one handle. Arnie poked its head round the door.

'Bad luck, Pan's scrawny kid. Word is you've got to go downstairs with the Lord of Hell. I'd pack your warm cloak. Gets chilly down there, so I hear.'

Demon set off back to the stables, Arnie loping beside him on its lion paws. He lugged the box behind him, bumping it over the rough earth as he ran. It let out an indignant squawk and four short legs appeared at its bottom corners.

'Emergency locomotion program in progress,' it squawked.

'Did I know you could do that?' Demon asked in surprise, stopping dead and letting go of the handle. The box bumped into him, knocking him over. 'Ouch!' he said. His knees were going to be permanently scabbed at this rate.

'That box is full of surprises,' said Arnie. 'Heffy gave it some upgrades, remember? Now come on. Hurry up. You have dragons to harness, and it doesn't do to keep Hades waiting. Not the most patient of gods, old Hellface.'

'But who's going to look after all of you lot?' Demon asked. 'I'm supposed to be the Official Beastkeeper to the Gods, but how can I do my job properly if I get taken away from Olympus by gods and goddesses?'

'Don't worry about that,' said Arnie. 'Doris will muck out if you offer it snackies of extra ambrosia. Beats me why it likes that disgusting stuff,' it added gloomily.

A short time later, Demon had given Doris the Hydra enough extra ambrosia cake to keep it happy for days. It had given him loving licks with its nine slimy green tongues and promised to keep the stables clean, and feed the other beasts till he returned. After that, he wrestled the harness onto two well-fed, happy dragons and led them up to where Hades was waiting in a swirl of impenetrable black mist, tapping one pointy black boot impatiently. The medical box followed closely at Demon's heels like a faithful dog.

'Hitch them up, ssstable boy, hitch them up,' said the Lord of the Underworld. So Demon closed his eyes, tugged on the reins and stepped forward into the darkness. As soon as the mist touched him, it felt like he was being pulled down into a neverending pit of grief, whose clammy depths clutched and clung to him, strangling all happiness. All the sad things that had ever happened in his life swirled through his head at once. The time the goat kid had fallen into the pond and drowned, the time he hadn't been able to save his favourite pet hen from the foxes, the time he'd found a wolf cub in a hunter's trap, his mother's heartbroken weeping as his dad stole him away forever . . . The blue-black metal reins dropped from his hand, tears poured down his cheeks as he stood, frozen to the spot.

'Ah,' said Hades. 'I'd forgotten about the wretched ssside-effect my pretty missst has on anyone who isssn't me. Here, boy, put thisss on and don't lossse it. You'll need it down below.' His gloved hand held out a ring, which seemed to be made of some kind of shiny black stone. 'And for Hermesss' sssake wipe your nose,' he went on. 'I don't want bogiesss sssmeared all over my nice chariot.'

Demon fumbled the ring onto his middle finger, where it settled, seeming to shrink and cling to his skin like a small band of cold fog. Immediately the feeling of sadness lifted, and as it did he noticed a chariot in front of him, made of the same blue-black metal as the harness. Fixed to it were two red lights in the shape of eyes. As Demon stepped closer to the chariot, they swivelled to watch him. The dragons had already backed themselves between the shafts, so he buckled the straps to hold them in, patted them on their knobbly flanks and turned to Hades.

'All ready, Your Fabulous Formidableness,'

Demon said, sounding almost cheerful in his relief at not feeling sad any more – not to mention avoiding being bitten or burned. He wiped his nose with the back of a grubby hand. The god shuddered slightly and held out a black handkerchief edged with black lace.

'Revolting boy,' he said, climbing into the driving scat. Demon made to follow him in, but Hades held up one black-gloved hand. 'Nuh-uh, ssstable boy! I travel alone. I'll sssee you down in the Underworld ssshortly. Mind the ghosssts on your way in from the gatesss.' With a darkly malevolent grin, he cracked a whip that seemed to be made of thin strands of blue lightning above the dragons' heads, and immediately they plunged downwards into the crack that had just opened at their feet.

Demon stared open-mouthed in shock as the red dragons'-eye lights on the chariot vanished and the crack snapped shut again as if it had never been. Did Hades really expect him to get to the gates of the Underworld all on his own?

Apparently the answer was yes.

# 4

# JOURNEY TO THE UNDERWORLD

'Oh,' said Demon finally, his mouth hanging open. 'But . . .' Arnie cackled behind him.

'Expecting a lift, were you, Pan's scrawny kid? Nope. You'll have to do it the normal way, get Charon the ferryman to row you across the Styx and all that. Mind you take a couple of coins for him – and a couple for the way back, if you're lucky enough to return. Go on, hurry up and hop on the Iris Express. She'll take you where you need to go. He wasn't joking when he said "Sssee you ssshortly", you know.' Arnie's imitation of Hades' sibilant voice was uncannily accurate.

Demon trudged back to his room to fetch four copper obols from his purse, and then over to the spot where the Iris Express usually landed, still followed by the box, which was staying remarkably silent. In his worry about what to say to Iris he totally forgot his warm cloak. He'd never summoned the goddess of the rainbow before.

'Er, Iris Express, please. For me and my box. To go to the gates of the Underworld,' he said nervously. There was a whoosh and a swish, and a rainbow arced down from the blue sky and landed in front of him.

'Unaccompanied minors and inanimate objects must belt up,' said a tinkly voice from just above the rainbow as Demon stepped inside. Immediately, multicoloured bands looped themselves around him and the box, pinning them both so they couldn't move. Demon's heart began to beat very fast, remembering his one and only trip on the Iris Express. He closed his eyes and gritted his teeth, waiting for the rainbow to plunge earthwards.

'Hold on, Iris,' said a light, cheerful voice. 'Wait for me.'

Demon opened his eyes. Standing in front of him was a tall, thin god with a mischievous smile on his face. Under one arm he carried a wide-brimmed hat, and he had a strange-looking carved staff in his hand, around which two golden snakes looped and turned in an endless figure of eight. Demon recognised Hermes, chief messenger of the gods, and stood up as straight as he could in the rainbow ropes.

'Good morning, Your gargantuan Godness,' he said politely. Hermes laughed.

'Hello, Pandemonius. No need for the flattery. Just plain Hermes will do,' he said. 'I'm not one of those gods who likes all that boring bowing and scraping. Now, I hear old Hades has snaffled you for some important medical work, and Hephaestus thought you might want a bit of company on the first bit of the road. Tricky place to get into, the Underworld. 'Specially since Heracles . . .' He pulled a face. 'Well, anyway, we're all relying on you to fix things down there.'

'Me? Fix things?' said Demon. He had a nasty

sinking feeling as he asked the next question. 'Er, what exactly am I supposed to fix? Hades just said he had a sick hound. What's that horrible Heracles gone and done now?' Demon had a serious grudge against Heracles, who was always trying to kill the immortal beasts.

Hermes laughed again. 'Sick hound? Oh, that's a good one. I never knew Uncle Hades had a sense of humour. He's certainly sick, but he's not *exactly* a hound. Anyway, you need to get there as quick as you can. I'm sure Hades will fill you in on what Heracles did when we arrive. Iris, take us down to that side gate no one uses any more. It's the fastest way in.'

With stomach-churning suddenness, the wisp of coloured nothingness dropped downwards, and Demon was suddenly concentrating too hard on not being sick to ask any more questions. Just as he thought he was going to lose the battle, there was a bump and a thump, the rainbow ropes loosened, and he fell forward. Hermes caught him with his strong arms just before Demon hit the ground and set him on his feet.

'Here we are,' the god said. 'Welcome to the side

gate of the Underworld – or Hell, as some of the Northerners like to call it.' They were outside the entrance to a very large cave. Long hanks of green-grey moss and old spiderwebs hung from its top and all around the sagging iron gates on both sides, making it look like an old man's toothless mouth surrounded by straggly silver whiskers. Although they stood in dim sunshine outside, from inside the cave seeped dark coils of mist that reached out and clung to Demon's and Hermes' feet and covered the silver box almost entirely. Demon felt them wrap around his ankles and drag him forward. Then they started to crawl up his legs, feeling their way like clammy fingers.

'Hey,' he yelled. 'Stop it!' He tried to run backwards, out of their grasp, but they clung even harder and worked their way up his body. Demon began to panic, thrashing about in his efforts to escape, but then the dank tendrils reached the hand wearing Hades's ring. Immediately the mist fingers shrivelled and shrank back into the cave-mouth.

'That's it,' said Hermes. 'Show them their Master's ring. I don't need one, but it should get you in and out of most places down here. All we have to do now is get past the angry ghosts.'

'A-a-angry ghosts?' Demon asked in a small voice. He didn't like the sound of that. 'Couldn't you just take me straight to Hades? Please, Hermes?'

'Now where would be the fun in that?' Hermes said. 'I'll get you past the ghosts, but then I've got to pop off and do a bit of business with some dead heroes. I'll give you one tip, though. Hephaestus told me to say that the box will help if you get into a tight spot. You just have to access the special features. Now come on. Doesn't do to keep Charon the ferryman waiting. Follow me!'

With a playful hoot of laughter, he darted forward into the darkness. Demon followed at a run. He had no choice – only Hermes knew the way, and he wasn't hanging about for Demon to catch up. The sole comfort he had was the silver box waddling and hopping along behind him, special features and all. Demon thought he could hear it panting. *Something* was breathing hard behind him, anyway. He shuddered and ran on after Hermes through the twisting loops and turns of the steep passage, too scared to look back, the god's staff giving out a faint greenish-golden light which reflected off black stone walls running with damp. There was a familiar smell of fusty-musty old dead things in the air, which got stronger and stronger the deeper into the earth they travelled. The light too got stronger and stronger the further down he went, but it wasn't coming from Hermes' staff. It was a sort of dead, flat twilight, which made it hard to pick out the details of anything too far away. Demon could hear a roaring noise up ahead, and suddenly he and Hermes burst out onto the banks of a midnight-black river, whose waters roiled and boiled and bubbled like a mad cauldron. On the other side was an enormous crowd of spectral grey shapes, running up and down, howling and moaning. Some were flinging themselves into the river, but as Demon watched, the churning water formed itself into lips that sucked them in and spat them back onto dry land. Some of the shapes were tearing at each other, ripping off arms and heads in a bloodless frenzy of viciousness, but as each ghostly limb or head dropped to the ground, it rose into the air and refixed itself to the spectral body it had come from. These ghosts were clearly very angry indeed.

'D-do we h-have to g-get through THEM?' Demon

stuttered. His legs and arms started to shake uncontrollably and his heart felt as if it was trying to climb out of his body. Being torn apart by furious ghosts while still alive would definitely be worse than being shrivelled into a heap of ash by a god, he thought.

'Yep,' said Hermes cheerfully. 'But don't worry. I have a trick or two up my godly sleeves.' Then he cupped his hands round his mouth. 'Oi! Charon, you old lazybones. Get that ferry over here double quick. Two passengers bound for Hades' palace.' He turned to Demon. 'Only Charon is allowed to take people over the River Styx, you know. Terrifying old beggar, but I guess living permanently on the borders of the realm of the dead will do that to a person.'

From the opposite bank, seemingly materialising out of nothing, glided a long black boat with a tall, hooded figure at the oars. Each oar rose and fell quite silently, dipping in and out of the now still water without so much as a splash, calming the river as it passed. As it slid in beside them, Hermes leapt lightly over the bow and held out a hand to Demon. 'On you get, young Pandemonius.'

The boat rocked slightly as he stepped on board,

then there was a thump as the silver box stumbled on behind Demon and fell heavily onto its side. 'System reboot, system reboot,' it said in a faint metallic shriek, blue sparks escaping from the slightly open lid. The small legs retracted, and with a click and a hiss the box fell silent. Demon had no time to worry about it, though, as scary Charon stood up and loomed over him, holding out a hand, palm upwards. It was a long, bony hand, almost fleshless, with yellow nails that curved like thick horny talons.

'Pay the ferryman,' he croaked. His voice sounded like rusty fishhooks sucked from rotting flesh. Demon fumbled desperately in the hanging pocket inside his chiton, and came out with two copper obols, dropping them in the ferryman's palm, trying not to touch the withered skin. Without another word Charon tossed the coins into the river. As they sank beneath the surface of the silent water he sat down, bent to his oars and started to row. The shrieking ghosts came nearer and nearer, and now Demon could see that they all had blood-red eyes and sharp, pointed teeth. Demon began to shake again. They were the scariest things he'd ever seen and he didn't want to be anywhere near them. He gave the water a desperate look. Maybe if he jumped in and swam downriver . . .

'Don't even think about it, Pandemonius,' said Hermes, giving him a sharp look and grabbing his arm. 'The waters of the Styx do strange things to half-mortals. You wouldn't want to end up serving Hades as a ghostly beetle-boy forever, now would you?'

Charon cackled inside his hood. It wasn't a friendly sound.

'N-no,' said Demon. 'But I also don't want to go anywhere near those horrible ghosts. Why are they so angry, anyway?'

'They're the souls of the murdered dead, seeking a way back to life to get revenge on their unpunished killers in the upper world,' said Hermes, letting go of him. 'Can't blame them, really, poor things, but I agree they're not very nice. Now, grab hold of the end of my staff in one hand and that box in the other, and be ready to move as soon as we hit the bank. The river won't stay calm for long. We'll need to be quick.'

Demon bent down to grab the handle of the box, which lay still and dead in the bottom of the boat.

'Any special features would be welcome right

about NOW,' he said hopefully.

The box woke up immediately, beeped once and began to flash silver and blue. 'Initiating solo pteranautics mode,' it said in its annoying tinny voice. Just as Demon tugged on the handle to try to lift it, it shot up off the floor of the boat, suddenly light as a feather, pulling Demon's arm up with it so he dangled from one hand, legs kicking in the empty air beneath him. Large bright blue wings erupted from its sides, flapping frantically as the box listed to one side under Demon's weight. The handle he was holding glowed bright red, burning his hand, and he let go with a yell and dropped heavily to the deck, sucking his fingers.

'Error code 781. Passenger mode disabled,' it beeped at Demon as he lay there, slightly stunned. The boat began to heave as the river woke up.

'Quick,' shouted Hermes again, his voice slightly frantic, holding out his staff to Demon. 'Grab hold.'

They hit the bank with a jolt and the angry ghosts began to swarm aboard the unsteady deck. Charon beat them off with his oars, laying about him left and right as he knocked them over the sides. Without even thinking, Demon launched himself at the messenger god's staff and seized it in both hands. The golden snakes wrapped themselves round his wrists, and suddenly they were zooming upwards, following the blue trails of sparks coming out of the now-flying silver box. Demon felt an icy cold hand wrench at his bare ankle, then it let go and they were soaring over the heads of the angry ghosts. Wails of rage followed them for what seemed like miles, but then quite suddenly they were gone, and Demon and Hermes were soaring downwards towards a barren landscape of pure silver-grey, still following the box. The god's sandals were just above Demon's head, and he saw that they had wings like the box, but these were white ones with golden tips. As Hermes landed the snakes unwrapped themselves and Demon was free, still slightly wobbly, but standing on his own two feet. He could hear an earthshaking noise far off to his left. It sounded like something sneezing its head off. A ginormous something. At each sneeze the ground trembled under his feet, and afterwards a dreadful howling filled the air.

'What's THAT?' Demon asked.

'THAT is your new patient,' Hermes replied.

'It definitely doesn't sound like a hound,' Demon said apprehensively. Anything that shook the earth when it sneezed was not going to be like any dog he'd every come across, that was for sure.

'Told you so,' said Hermes. Then he sniffed the air. 'This is where I say goodbye and good luck,' he said. 'I smell the lovely graveyard whiff of my uncle over that hill, and he doesn't really approve of me. He's a bit allergic to my fun and jokes, old Hades, so I need to stay well away from him. Also, he's jealous of my hat. The palace is that way.' Putting a hand on Demon's shoulder, he pointed to a small path between the rocks, leading uphill. 'Adios, kid. We're all relying on you to cure that beast. Remember, whatever happens, DON'T EAT ANYTHING DOWN HERE.' He banged his hat against his thigh and grinned at Demon. 'Good old invisibility hat – my trusty friend in time of trouble.' Then he put it on and disappeared, flashing out of sight between one word and the next.

Hermes had vanished, and the silver box had just flapped over the horizon. Demon's stomach lurched towards his toes. He was all alone in the Underworld.

# 5
# THE GUARDIAN
# OF THE UNDERWORLD

Demon set off at a run, scrambling up and over the pale rocks. Now he too could smell the unmistakeable reek of the god of death wafting towards him on the still air. As he reached the top of the hill and began to run down the other side, he saw an extraordinary sight. Immediately below him stood a vast palace built of smooth shiny black granite flecked with silver, every tower, turret and spire crowned with a rotating silver skull with ruby eyes. High walls enclosed the palace, so high that he couldn't see over them. And there, lying chained in front of a massive pair of closed silver gates in the left-hand wall, was a beast such as he'd never seen before. It had a dog's body, three gigantic dog heads, each crowned with a hissing mane of differently coloured snakes, a long, thick serpent tail and lion's paws, each tipped with needle-sharp golden claws. Hovering near it was the winged box, and beside it stood Hades, arms folded and glowering like a furious black cloud.

'A-AA-A-A-AA-A-CCCCHHHHHOOOOO OO! AAARRRROOOOOOOO!'

'A-AA-A-A-AA-A-CCCCHHHHHOOOOO OO! AAARRRROOOOOOOO!'

'A-AA-A-A-AA-A-CCCCHHHHHOOOOO OO! AAARRRROOOOOOOO!'

Each of the beast's heads sneezed and howled over and over again in a thunderous chorus, thumping and thudding on the ground, cracks appearing all round where it lay. It was clearly exhausted.

'You're late, ssstable boy,' Hades growled. 'Come here NOW.'

Stumbling and sliding over the trembling ground,

Demon forced his wobbly legs to take him towards the angry god. If the poor beast hadn't been there he might have turned and fled, but the sight of the huge hound lying on its side, sneezing its three heads off, and the sudden worry about what Heracles might have done to it, made him braver.

'I-I'm sorry, Your High Hellishness. I got here as soon as I could.' He dared to look up at Hades. 'What is this beast, Your M-m-m-ajestic M-mightiness? And what's the matter with it?' At least it was still visibly alive and had all its heads attached, he thought. Unlike what Heracles had done to the poor Hydra.

Hades looked a tiny bit less cross when he heard the obvious concern in Demon's voice. But not much. Steam was drifting out of his ears, and his eyes were glowing red.

'Thisss,' he said, 'is Cerberusss, my Guardian Hound of the Underworld. That oaf Heraclesss beat him up in a fight – and then he put a diamond chain round hisss neck and dragged him up to earth. He'sss never been the sssame sssince. It'sss all my wretched sssister Hera'sss fault for giving Heraclesss sssuch a ssstupid tasssk. Now my poor hound is USSSELESSS.'

He spat, and where the spittle landed, it hissed and smoked. Demon cringed back slightly. He really really didn't want to be in the middle of a fight between a frightening god and an even more terrifying goddess. But then Hades beckoned him closer, and as Demon edged towards him nervously, he snapped open a small window in the silver gates. 'Look through here, ssstable boy, and sssee what happensss when the Underworld has no guardian.'

Demon went on tiptoes and peered through the window. He gasped. Some way away, on a flat plain covered in white flowers stretching as far as the eye could see, were thousands and thousands of figures, not just ghosts (though there were masses of those) but a few real live humans too, who were wandering about, pointing and chattering behind a man with a red placard on a stick.

'That idiot Heraclesss left the upper gate open – my personal, private gate, which bypassesss Charon and the Ssstyx. Now we have humansss here. LIVING HUMANSSS!' The god's voice rose to a roar which made the ground tremble. 'There's a man called Georgiosss running TOURSSS! "Meet Your Favourite

Hero" he's selling it as, up there on earth. And Brother Zeusss hasss forbidden me to do ANYTHING about it till YOU make Cerberusss better!'

'He won't ssstop sssneezing and howling,' the Lord of the Underworld went on. 'And he'sss doing it ssso loud and ssso often that the foundationsss of my kingdom are SSSTARTING TO CRACK!' He gestured towards the largest rift. 'Ssseee, ssstable boy?' he hissed. Demon looked, trying to keep his balance as Cerberus sneezed and howled again and the ground swayed like a ship's deck underneath his feet. The rock at the bottom of the cleft was moving too, roiling and rippling – almost as if something was trying to get through.

'I-it doesn't look good, Your Infernal Immortalness,' Demon said, timidly.

'DOESSSN'T LOOK GOOD!' Hades roared. 'That'sss Tartarusss down there! TARTARUSSS!'

Demon nearly let out a terrified squeak. Tartarus was where the horrible hundred-armed monsters were imprisoned. The ones who'd tried to defeat the gods. The ones who ate all the poo he shovelled down the chute from the stables.

Hades bent his head closer. 'You ssseee the problem, ssstable boy,' he said in a scary whisper. 'If thossse hundred-armed monstersss essscape, they'll dessstroy the whole world. Sssooo . . .' There was an ominous pause. Demon closed his eyes and braced himself. He pretty much knew what came next when a god was this cross.

Hades seized Demon by the shoulders and drew him even closer, so that the god's grave-dirt breath washed over him like a foul wave. 'You've got one day to find out what'sss wrong with my guardian, ssstable boy, and cure him,' he hissed. 'Or I asssure you, I'll tie you to a bigger fiery wheel than Ixion, ssspin you till you're dizzy and roassst your toesss to cindersss. That'sss jussst for ssstartersss. After that I'll let my army of ssskeleton ghossst dragonsss chassse you and eat you over and over again for the ressst of your wretched mortal daysss . . . which I can make asss long as I pleassse! How would you like THAT?'

Before Demon could answer that he wouldn't like it at all, Hades threw him to the ground with a thump and strode off into the palace, its black stone doors slamming behind him with the sound of a funeral knell. Demon lay there, wheezing, trying to get his breath back. Offy and Yukus slithered off his collar and curled around his bruises, soothing them so that he was able to get to his feet again.

*Wretched gods*, he thought, not daring to say it out loud in case Hades heard him. Why did they always have to be so violent? He'd have tried his hardest to cure poor Cerberus anyway, without being threatened with such awful punishments. Did Hades really think that scaring him was going to help? He sighed, trying not to think of how roasted toes and being in several skeletal dragon stomachs would feel, and went over to his patient.

Cerberus's three noses were red and running with yellow slime, and its six eyes were swollen nearly shut. The multicoloured snakes that made up his manes sneezed continuously in a faint hissing chorus, punctuated by enormous volcanic *atishoos* from the three heads. Demon stroked Cerberus's rough dog's fur.

'Poor old chap,' he said. 'We'll get you well again.'

Cerberus groaned weakly in between sneezes and howls. Then his six puffy eyes swivelled to look at

Demon out of inflamed slits. 'Thank you, Pan's son,' growled the first head. The second head nodded, and the serpent tail thudded weakly on the ground. 'I think my old bones might shake to pieces if you don't get me better soon.' The third head and the snakes just moaned and hissed pitifully, then all the eyes closed.

Demon turned to the box. 'I need you,' he said, 'and none of your stupid word games. This is an emergency.' He was determined not to take any of its usual nonsense this time.

The box flapped over and settled down beside him. Demon opened its lid, and the familiar blue symbols glowed up at him. 'Tell me what's wrong with this beastdog,' Demon commanded it. At once three cotton swabs on flexible metal arms poked out. Working quickly, they rubbed around the hellhound's six nostrils and took samples of the yellow slime, then retracted, disappearing in a flash of silver light.

'Running diagnostics . . . running diagnostics . . . running diagnostics . . .' said the familiar metallic voice. Then there was a pause and a loud whirring sound. Then, 'Tricephalic helionosos,' said the box, in its usual smug way. Demon felt like kicking it.

'Stupid thing,' he said, too cross to be polite. 'I TOLD you not to do that. Say it so that I can understand.'

'Sun,' said the box quickly, flapping out of his way.

'What do you mean, "sun"?' asked Demon. 'Sun isn't an illness, is it?'

'Do I really have to spell it out?' sighed the box. 'Patient is allergic to Helios's rays. Must have had too much exposure when he was up top with Heracles. It's given him a permanent case of sneezes and earache in all three heads, as well as swelling every eye shut. He can't see, he can't hear properly, and he definitely can't do any guarding.'

'Well, we need to cure him,' said Demon. 'Within a day. Or me and my toes will be on a fiery wheel quicker than you can say chill on the chest, not to mention the skeleton ghost dragons eating me forever and ever.'

The box buzzed and hummed. Then it buzzed and hummed some more. The blue symbols flickered.

'Come ON,' said Demon. He looked down at his

ten dirty toes and then over to the black door of Hades' palace. He had the uneasy feeling that something horrible was going to come out of it at any minute. 'Hurry UP!'

The blue symbols turned a vile sickly green, and a small crystal bottle rose out of the box's depths.

'Temporary stasis cure. Apply one drop to each eyelid and in each nostril,' it said, tinnily.

Demon seized the bottle, hurried over to the huge body and started to do as the box had told him. The drops smelled of honey. As soon as he had finished, Cerberus heaved three huge sighs, one from each head, rolled over, and stopped breathing. Demon nearly stopped breathing too.

'WHAT HAVE YOU DONE, YOU STUPID THING?' Demon yelled at the silver medicine box as he frantically felt around the unmoving beast's chest for a heartbeat. Where would it be? On the left? On the right?

The box flapped hurriedly out of the way. 'Bought you time,' it squawked sulkily. 'That's what a stasis potion does. It'll keep the patient in limbo and stop him sneezing for a bit. That'll just about give you time to get the ingredients I need to make the proper cure before Hades comes after you.'

'Ingredients? What ingredients?' asked Demon, finally giving up on trying to find Cerberus's pulse. The box ticked and clicked, then spat out a piece of parchment with brightly coloured pictures on it at Demon's feet. He bent and picked it up.

'Great,' he muttered. 'Some kind of yellow flower I've never seen before. Those are spider's webs and that's grass of Parnassus. But what's that coming out of the lyre thingy, and what's the wobbly square picture and the one that looks like some dopey girl's head with air coming out and that pot thing?'

'Three wolfsbane petals, a fingerful of spiderweb, seven grass of Parnassus flowers, the toenail of a hero, a maiden's sigh, the high and low notes from a lyre – and a Cauldron of Healing.'

As the box rattled off the impossible-sounding list, Demon's heart sank lower and lower. A maiden's sigh? A hero's toenail? Notes from a lyre? And what in the name of Athene's knickers was wolfsbane? He'd never heard of it. How was he ever supposed to find any of those down here, let alone a Cauldron of

Healing – whatever that was? It was a totally impossible task.

Demon slumped to the ground despairingly beside Cerberus's still body, put his head in his hands and groaned. He might as well call Hades to toast his toes now and have done with it, he thought. But just then, a cautious whisper came through the small window in the silver gates.

'Pandemonius, hey, Pandemonius! Are you there?' Demon raised his head. Only the gods called him Pandemonius – and his mother when she was cross. It couldn't be his mother – could it? No matter how much he'd like to see her, he really, really hoped it wasn't. Maybe Hermes had come back to help him. He got up slowly and went over to the gates, not daring to hope. When he peered through the window, though, he saw nothing nearby except some wisps of white mist. Maybe Hermes was still wearing his invisibility hat.

'Who's there?' he whispered back. 'Hermes, is that you?'

'No, silly, it's me, Orpheus.'

Demon frowned. There'd been an Orpheus his

mother had told him about – some young musician boy who'd defied Hades for the sake of love. It was kind of a soppy story, and he hadn't paid much attention. Now he wished he had. He still couldn't see anybody, though, craning his neck to left and right to peer through the small gap.

'Where are you?' Demon asked. Then he stared. Gradually the wisps of mist were forming into a shape right in front of his eyes. The shape of a teenage boy, carrying some kind of musical instrument under his arm. A musical instrument? Could it be? Demon stared hard. A curving frame like two cow horns, with strings in between them . . .

'Is that a lyre?' he asked eagerly.

'Yes,' said Orpheus, still a bit see-through but now fully visible. 'It is. Now come on through the gate. Quick! I don't want Hades to catch me here!'

'Er, it's Demon, really,' said Demon. 'Calling me Pandemonius makes me feel like I'm in trouble.'

'Well, you will be if you don't get through that gate RIGHT NOW!' Orpheus whispered urgently.

# 6

# THE BOY WITH
# THE LYRE

Demon was a bit worried. After all, he didn't know
Orpheus from a bar of Melanie the naiad's soap. And
what about leaving Cerberus? But the box assured
him that the Guardian of the Underworld would
come to no harm.

'What if Hades comes out and sees him like this?'
Demon asked, hesitating.

'Then you're better off not here, aren't you?' said

the box in its metallic voice. 'Now HURRY UP. Like Orpheus said, the clock is ticking and you only have a day to find my ingredients, or there won't BE a cure.'

A few moments later, after a bit of fiddling with the latch and some hard pushing, the silver gates creaked open, and Demon walked quickly through to the other side, closing them gently behind him with a last look back at his enormous beast-dog patient, who hadn't so much as twitched a claw since he'd been given the stasis potion. He just hoped the box was right and that Cerberus wasn't actually dead. It came up behind him and hovered at his shoulder, wings flapping gently, and they both went towards the ghostly figure pacing up and down impatiently among the white flowers. The red-eyed silver skulls on top of the palace swivelled to watch the two of them walk out onto the plain and then turned away.

Now Demon was truly in the land of the dead. He secretly checked his body to see that it was still solid and human. Luckily it was. Then he took a deep breath and looked around him properly for the first time. The dim twilight covered the landscape, making everything soft and blurred, as if nothing was quite real. The sky (if it was a sky) had no clouds, no stars, nor any moon, but glowed a kind of eerie green as far as the eye could see. There were no birds, only flocks of ghostly bats chittering and squeaking overhead. The white flowers were everywhere, their spiky heads covering the ground like a carpet.

'Could you go a bit further away?' Orpheus asked the box as it flapped near him. 'Only it's quite hard to hold this shape together in a breeze.' Bits of him swirled and reformed as the wafts of air touched his misty body. It was very disconcerting to watch. The box thumped down to the floor beside Demon, and as its wings furled and then vanished, its four stumpy legs reappeared.

'Locomotion mode resumed. Happy now?' it grumbled.

'Yes, much better, thank you,' Orpheus said, ignoring its grouchy tone of voice. Demon ignored it too. He had more important things on his mind.

'How did you know I was here?' he burst out. He was really longing to know whether Orpheus could still play the lyre in his present form, but hesitated to ask. He'd never had a conversation with a ghost before, and he didn't want to say the wrong thing.

'Hermes said you were down here and might need a bit of assistance,' Orpheus said. 'Though I'm not sure how I can help, really.'

Demon sent a barrowload of thankful thoughts in Hermes' direction. 'Well, I can think of one thing right away,' he said. Never mind politeness, he had to know. 'Does your lyre still work?' he blurted out.

'Of course it does,' said Orpheus, sounding slightly offended, as Demon had feared he would. 'I may be dead, but I'm still the world's greatest musician, you know.' He pulled out the curved instrument and strummed his fingers over the strings. The loveliest trill of music rose up into the air as Demon hurried to explain about the two lyre notes on the impossible list of ingredients he needed to find to help cure Cerberus.

'But how will you catch them?' asked Orpheus.

'Oh,' Demon said. It simply hadn't occurred to him that he might need to actually catch the notes. He looked down at the box. 'Any clever ideas, Oh Mighty Chest of Wisdom?' he asked.

The box didn't answer. It just stomped over to Orpheus and shot out a sort of trumpet-shaped thing on a long tube, somehow fastening itself onto the frame of the misty lyre like an octopus's sucker. 'Play a D and an E,' it instructed Orpheus.

The musician plucked two strings. The first note thrummed so low that Demon felt it vibrate deep in his bellybutton. The second was so high that it set his back teeth on edge. As the two notes died, the trumpet thing made a slurping noise and belched in a satisfied way.

'Musical items retrieved and saved to disc,' said the box, as the trumpet detached itself from the lyre and wavered back inside the lid. One ingredient down, five more and a magic cauldron to go, Demon thought. Suddenly his stomach began to rumble loudly, and he realised he was very hungry. It seemed a very long time since he'd had sausage in a bun in Hestia's kitchens.

'Oh dear,' said Orpheus. 'I'd forgotten humans need food. That's too bad.'

'What do you mean?' Demon asked.

'Well,' said Orpheus. 'You mustn't eat anything

down here. That's how Hades caught his wife, Queen Persephone. She only ate seven pomegranate seeds, and now she has to stay down here for four months of every year. You can't let even one thing pass your lips until you return to the upper world, or you'll be Hades' prisoner forever.'

Demon suddenly remembered that Hermes had told him the same thing. He decided to ignore his stomach, however much it complained. He definitely didn't want to be Hades' prisoner for one single minute, let alone forever.

'Now show me that list,' said Orpheus, holding out his insubstantial hand. Demon took the list out of the folds of his chiton and handed it over at once. Unfortunately it seemed that ghosts couldn't hold mortal things. The piece of parchment slipped right through Orpheus's fingers and drifted to the ground. Demon picked it up and held it out so that the ghostly boy could see the pictures.

'Hmm. Spiderwebs are easy – Arachne has lots. Then grass of Parnassus grows by the banks of the River Lethe, just where it joins the marsh. I'm not sure about this yellow flower, but Eurydice will know.'

'Who's Eurydice?' Demon interrupted. Orpheus's see-through cheeks took on a slightly pink shade, as if Eos had just touched him with her fingers.

'Er, she's my girlfriend,' he muttered. 'Hades is always forbidding us to be together, but we don't take much notice . . . that's why I don't want him to catch me here.' He cast a very nervous glance back at the silver skulls on top of the palace. 'Anyway,' he went on in a rush, changing the subject quickly, 'let's start with the hero's toenail. That shouldn't be too hard. There must be at least a thousand of them down here, and it doesn't say it has to be a live hero, does it?'

'No,' said Demon, 'it doesn't. But where . . .?' He broke off, suddenly noticing that the crowds of people and ghosts he'd seen when Hades had made him look through the window of the gate were drifting towards them over the plain. There was a lot of noise going on, and the sound of a man shouting. 'Might there be a hero in that lot?' he asked.

'Almost certainly,' said Orpheus. 'Follow me. And try not to get trampled in the crush following that wretched Georgios.'

Orpheus shot forward, the bottom half of his

body dissolving into a long streamer of mist as he did so. Demon sprinted in his wake, with the box galloping clumsily behind. He felt a bit nervous. He hadn't met a hero before. Were they as scary as gods and goddesses? *Surely not*, he thought as he ran over the white flower spikes, crushing them under his feet so that a sickly sweet perfume rose into the air. Heroes were meant to be on the side of good, weren't they? Then he remembered Heracles. Heracles called himself a hero, so maybe that wasn't true after all.

Just as he was pondering this, they reached the crowd and Demon crashed hard into the tall man called Georgios who Hades had pointed out earlier. Up close he had a very large stomach and enormous, extremely dirty feet. He was also the one they had heard shouting. All thought of heroes was knocked out of Demon's head as he fell over with a bump, right on top of the box.

'Oof! Operating system overload! Operating system overload!' it squawked, spitting blue sparks. Demon got up hurriedly. He couldn't afford for it to go wrong. There was no Heffy down here to fix it.

'What's this, what's this?' said a loud voice above

him, as he struggled to his feet. 'I don't remember you being on my tour. Have you sneaked in without paying? Can't have that, can I?' said Georgios, waving his red placard, which Demon now saw had a picture of a snake and a skull on it, with a pair of crossed swords.

'No,' said Demon, indignant at the accusation. 'I haven't. I'm on a job for Hades, if you must know.'

The man laughed. 'A likely story,' he said. 'A little shrimp like you on a job for His Majesty the God of Death? I don't think so, sonny. And what's that you've got there? Stolen it, have you?' He reached down for the box, but as his fingers touched it, it let out a huge orange flash of lightning, which made the man snatch his hand away with a shriek.

'Oops! Error code 93. That wasn't supposed to happen,' said the box. It didn't sound very sorry, though. For once Demon felt like patting it.

'Perhaps that'll teach you to believe people when they're telling the truth,' he said. Georgios backed away, sucking his burnt hand. He gave Demon a nasty look, waved his red placard over his head and walked off muttering. Then he began to shout again.

'Come along, people! Come along! Follow

Georgios's Underworld Tours sign! Best and only one in the business! Next stop, Achilles and Ajax. Have your hero autograph books at the ready.' A chattering crowd of humans fell in behind the man, as Demon began to look for Orpheus. There was such a press of ghosts and people around him that he couldn't see the musician boy at all. He began to panic, but then caught sight of a misty lyre, held up high over everyone's heads, waving wildly. He began to run towards it, pushing his way between ghostly figures, who melted and flowed round him (and sometimes through him) as he went, leaving him cold and shivering. He wished he'd taken Arnie's advice and brought his cloak. Finally he got through to Orpheus.

'We'll never find anyone in this crowd,' shouted the ghost. 'Georgios's tours are making this bit of the Underworld a nightmare. Come this way!'

After more pushing and shoving, and a lot more walking they came to a dead tree, where several warrior ghosts wearing armour and carrying spears and swords were gathered. With them was a gigantic man with a misty bow on his back, a belt made of faintly shining stars, and a mass of ghostly hounds round his feet.

'There's your hero ghost,' said Orpheus.

'Is that Orion?' whispered Demon. Orpheus nodded, so Demon marched up to him bravely. Orion had been killed by the Giant Scorpion, Demon's least favourite beast in the stables on Olympus. Although Orion was a hunter, and he didn't normally like hunters, Demon had some sympathy for the dead hero. He'd been stung by the Giant Scorpion too. It hurt a lot.

'Excuse me, Your Extreme Heroicness,' he said. 'But could I have one of your toenails, please?' All the warrior ghosts laughed.

'You human souvenir-hunters!' one of them said. 'Bits from ghosts never last up in the mortal world, you know!'

'I'm not a souvenir-hunter,' said Demon crossly. 'I'm the Official Beastkeeper to the Gods. I need a hero's toenail for a potion to cure Cerberus.'

'Ah,' said Orion. 'Poor old Cerberus. We heard what happened. It's been chaos down here ever since. Well, if that's what it's for, you can certainly have one, Beastkeeper.'

Orion shooed the ghost dogs away, bent down to his left foot and pulled one of his large square toenails right off, making ghostly blood ooze onto his sandal. He didn't even wince at the pain. Immediately, a pair of pincers came out of the box and grabbed it.

'Toenail item recovered,' it trilled happily.

'Thanks, Orion,' Demon said gratefully, trying not to look at the misty blood pooling under the hero's foot. Then he had a thought. 'Er, do you know where we could find a maiden's sigh by any chance?' he asked. Orion and the others sniggered.

'Orpheus here will help you with that,' he said, winking. 'He's got a few maidens sighing after him.'

Orpheus blushed again. 'Shhh!' he said. 'Stop teasing me. You know there's only one I care about. Come on, Demon, let's go and find Eurydice.'

*Just five things to go now*, Demon thought, as they walked away from the laughing warriors. Maybe he could do this in one day after all.

It took ages to reach the grove where Eurydice lived, but they got there at last. Eurydice was a tall, beautiful girl ghost with long hair down to her knees. Getting her to sigh into the box's trumpet attachment turned out to be easy. She just had to look at Orpheus. Demon stared at the two of them in disgust while they hugged and kissed as if they hadn't seen each other for years. He didn't get this being-in-love thing at all. It was really soppy and embarrassing.

'Ahem,' Demon said at last, clearing his throat loudly in an obvious kind of way. 'Spiderwebs? Wolfsbane petals? Grass of Parnassus? Cauldron of Healing?' The two lovers took absolutely no notice of him, gazing into each others' eyes goopily.

'I STILL NEED FOUR THINGS TO CURE CERBERUS!' he yelled at last. Both Orpheus and Eurydice jumped a foot into the air and then dissolved into streamers of mist.

'Don't *do* that!' said Orpheus's voice indistinctly. 'I thought Hades had caught us for a minute. Now we'll have to disentangle ourselves.' Tapping his foot impatiently, Demon waited while the two lovers sorted themselves out.

'Now,' he said. 'Are you going to help me find the other things or not?'

# 7

# THE SPINNER'S CAVE

'Ooh!' said Eurydice, clapping her ghostly hands as she looked at Demon's list. They made no sound. 'That's Cerberus's new flower!'

'Cerberus's new flower? What do you mean?'

'It was when Heracles was dragging him back down here from earth,' said Eurydice. 'I was coming out of Arachne's cave, and I saw them. Wherever Cerberus's drool touched the ground, little yellow flowers sprang up, just like buttercups. They were so pretty. I've never seen a colour like that down here before. It's all horrid old grey and black and that icky green colour the sky is.'

'Could you take me to where they're growing?' Demon asked eagerly.

Eurydice made a face. 'It's a long way. And Arachne was quite mean to me last time I visited.'

'We need to get some spiderweb from Arachne, anyway,' said Orpheus. 'She's only mean because she has all those arms and legs now. It was so horrid of Athena to turn her into a spider. We don't have to go the long way, there's always the shortcut past Lethe's marsh. Come on, it's important. Like a hero's quest or something.'

'Please,' begged Demon. He was very aware of the clock ticking away. He wriggled his toes uncomfortably.

'Oh, all right,' said Eurydice. 'I don't mind Arachne really. But don't blame me if Lethe gets you. She's really scary. We'll have to try to go past really quietly without her noticing.'

Some time later they were trudging along in silent single file along a squelchy grey path beside a marsh. Demon tried to ignore his grumbling stomach. He was so hungry he would have eaten dirt if someone had given him a plate of it. *Mustn't eat mustn't eat mustn't eat* was the monotonous refrain that accompanied his heavy footsteps. It was all very disheartening. There was almost no one about in this part of the Underworld, apart from the ever-present ghost bats. Demon liked bats. There'd been a colony near his home in Arcadia. As he craned his head upwards, trying to listen to what they were saying to take his mind off his stomach, he tripped over his own feet and fell on his hands and knees into the marshy water. There was a sudden stink of old, unwashed socks.

'Ugh,' he spluttered. Just as he had begun to scramble out, a bony hand grabbed his wrist, nails digging into his flesh like claws.

'Not so fast,' said a harsh voice, bubbling up from under the water. Eurydice moaned with terror and hid behind Orpheus, who was holding his lyre like a weapon. Demon shook his wrist over and over again, trying to get free, but it was no good. The hand had him in a grip like an iron vice. Then the marsh plopped and bubbled as a terrible figure rose up from the water, draped in slimy grey waterweed robes. Her beautiful face was as pale as the moon, and her eyes burned with a faint blue fire.

'What do we have here?' the figure snarled through a mouth full of sharp pointed teeth. 'A mortal boy, two ghosts and . . .' she peered over Demon's shoulder, 'a silver box with legs?'

Demon's heart was pounding like one of Hephaestus's hammers. This must be Lethe, spirit of forgetfulness. 'I-I-I'm sorry, Your Magnificent Marshiness,' he stuttered. Lethe smiled at him. It was not a nice smile.

'Ohhhh! You WILL be,' she said. 'You'll be sorrier than a squashed scorpion.' She began to pull him down into the marsh once more. Demon felt himself begin to sink.

'Noooo!' he wailed. 'Orpheus, help me!'

At that moment Orpheus began to play his lyre. Then he began to sing. It was the saddest song Demon had ever heard. As the sorrowful notes wove round them, Lethe's grip slackened and Demon scrabbled backwards towards the path as fiery blue tears started to run down her cheeks, setting the oily surface of the water aflame.

'Ahh!' she sighed. 'Now you've spoiled all my fun, Orpheus. You know I can't resist your music.' Orpheus kept on playing as Demon hauled himself out and tried to scrape the grey ooze off himself as best he could. He wasn't very successful and his chiton flapped wetly round his legs. When Orpheus's song came to an end, Lethe took a gliding step towards them through the burning water. Demon cowered back. Eurydice was right. She was very scary indeed.

'Oh, do stop cringing, boy,' she said irritably. 'Tell me why you were creeping past my marsh like a thief in the night.' Demon explained about Cerberus, his voice still trembling slightly.

'Very well,' said Lethe. 'For Cerberus's sake I will let you pass this time. But if you ever come this way again, I shall demand a price. I will take your most precious memory from you. It will not be a pleasant experience.' Demon nodded. He was so desperate to leave he would have agreed to anything to get out of there. He'd just noticed that the sky had grown a little darker. How long did he have before his day ran out? Then he noticed that Lethe was holding a bunch of delicate five-petalled white flowers out to him. 'You may need these,' she said.

Behind him, the box opened its lid.

'Insert floral items here, please,' it said, sounding more polite than Demon had ever heard it. He pushed the flowers carefully into the opening. 'Grass of Parnassus accepted,' said the box, and snapped shut again. Demon felt a little more cheerful. Now there were only three things left to find for the potion.

As they left Lethe behind, Eurydice was full of how brave and clever Orpheus had been. She went on and on about it as Demon stumbled on over the now stony path and up the high rocky hills that led to Arachne's cave. He wished Eurydice would shut up, but he knew he needed her to show him where Cerberus's flowers were, so he didn't say so. Finally, as they came over a small rise, he saw a bright patch of yellow on the hillside above.

'That's them!' Eurydice cried.

Demon raced up the hill, panting and slipping in his eagerness, picked three yellow petals, and brought them back down to the box, which was ready and waiting beside Orpheus and Eurydice.

'Insert –'

'I know,' said Demon. 'Insert floral items here. I'm not stupid, you know.'

'Could have fooled me,' muttered the box crossly, trailing along behind the three of them as they continued climbing higher and higher up the mountainside, towards Arachne's cave. Suddenly, Demon began to feel a stickiness under his feet. *Schlurp schlap schlurp* went his sandals. He looked down. Trails of thick slime covered the path.

'What's this?' he asked, a bit too loudly.

'Hush,' said Eurydice. 'You'll soon see. But don't mention it in front of Arachne. She doesn't like to talk about it.' The stickiness got worse as they reached the entrance to the cave. Demon could hear a regular clicking and clunking sound coming from inside.

Orpheus rang a little bell that hung outside.

'Who's there?' said a silvery kind of voice.

'It's us, Orpheus and Eurydice,' said Orpheus. 'And we've brought someone to see you.'

'Come in then,' said Arachne. 'And mind the tapestries on the floor.'

As Demon stepped after the others into the cave, his eyes nearly bugged right out of his head. There in front of him crouched an enormous grey spider, her eight legs busy weaving on four different looms, shuttles flying faster than his eye could see. There was a mass of different coloured threads spooling out from her spinnerets – along with a lot of sticky stuff, which covered the whole floor with a thick, gluey coating. What was even odder was that the spider had the face of a pretty girl.

From each loom hung beautiful tapestry pictures of all the gods and goddesses. There was Zeus with his thunderbolts, there was Hera with her peacocks – and there was Heffy at his forge. They were all slightly irreverent, though. Zeus was wearing a silly hat, Hera was covered in peacock poo and Heffy was using a chicken instead of a hammer.

'Wow!' Demon said. 'They're amazing! You must be very brave to weave those!'

It was just the right thing to say. Arachne beamed, obviously not in a mean mood today, despite Eurydice's fears.

'Ooh!' she squealed. 'How nice of you to say so.'

Then she frowned. 'But how does a mortal boy come to be down here?'

Demon explained about Cerberus yet again.

'All we need now are some, er, spiderwebs,' he said. 'And a Cauldron of Healing.'

'Help yourself to webs,' said Arachne, gesturing with one spindly leg to the corner. 'I've plenty to spare.' So Demon gathered up a fingerful of the multicoloured thread, getting himself hopelessly stuck together as he did so. The box clearly didn't like having sticky feet so it had taken to the air again, wings flapping. Orpheus and Eurydice huddled away from the gusts of air, trying to keep their bodies together as two long mechanical arms appeared from under the box's wings and unravelled Demon, turning him round and round as it coiled the spiderweb strands into a neat rope.

'Web item retrieved and stored to memory,' its tinny voice said.

'Did you say you needed a Cauldron of Healing?' Arachne asked, when Demon was slightly less stuck together.

Demon nodded. 'Do you know where I could find one?'

'We-e-e-ll,' said Arachne slowly. 'I'd normally send you up to Chiron the centaur in the mortal world. But down here . . .' She shook her head, and Demon's heart sank into his sandals again.

'Do you think Queen Persephone might have one?' Orpheus asked. 'She's a healer, isn't she?'

Suddenly Eurydice started jumping up and down. Her misty feet didn't stick to the floor at all, Demon noticed as he picked bits of web out of his hair and fingernails. Perhaps there were some benefits to being a ghost.

'You're so clever, Orphy! I think I've seen one in her chambers,' she squealed. 'That time Hades made me be her lady-in-waiting, when he was first trying to keep us apart, remember? She made a potion in it to mend one of the Skeleton Guard's arms. Might it be a little golden cauldron with a silver handle?' she asked the box, which was now hovering in the cave entrance.

'Affirmative,' it said.

'D-does that mean I have to go into Hades' palace?' asked Demon, dreading the answer, and wondering nervously what a Skeleton Guard was.

'I'm afraid it does,' said Orpheus. 'And I don't think you've got much time left. Look – the day is coming to an end.' He gestured at the cave entrance.

Demon looked outside. It was much darker.

'Two hours three minutes and twenty seconds, two hours three minutes and nineteen seconds, two hours three minutes and eighteen seconds,' the box chimed in helpfully.

Demon glared at it.

'Let's get going, then,' he said through gritted teeth.

# 8

# THE PALACE OF DEATH

It was one of the most uncomfortable journeys of Demon's entire life. The box had grudgingly agreed to enable its special passenger mode for him, even providing a large bottle for Orpheus to pour himself into, so he didn't blow away during the ride. After many tearful farewells from Eurydice, who was staying with Arachne for a while longer, Demon lay lengthways on the box's silver lid, clinging onto Orpheus's bottle with one hand and the box's handle with the other. Its large blue wings flapped frantically, once, twice, three times and then they were airborne.

'Goodbye, Orphy!' sobbed Eurydice.

'Good luck, Demon!' called Arachne.

Demon slipped and slid from side to side, terrified he was going to fall off as the box laboured across Lethe's marsh and then veered sharply right.

'Watch out,' he yelled, as a cloud of ghostly bats flew straight at them. The box plunged downwards, dropping so low that Demon's toes scuffed and scraped along the stony ground.

'Ow! Ow! Ow!' he howled, as he felt the skin on his feet grate away, but the box merely let out a stream of blue symbols which streamed past his ears, crackling and spitting with sparks. §⌘❂✖ΘΧξϖ*Ψ✗v÷∞¶x**n)£@Σ□φ∠*∈⊇♠ℑ, it panted, rising into the air again with an alarming wobble which made him nearly drop Orpheus's bottle.

Over Eurydice's grove, over the warriors' tree, over crowded plain of ghosts they flew, until Demon could see the black walls of Hades' palace glittering in front of him. With one last, mighty effort, the box heaved itself and Demon over the silver gates and flumped down beside Cerberus's body with a crash. As Demon thudded to the ground, the silver skulls on top of the palace roofs swivelled to look at him, fiery eyes suddenly igniting, so that he was suddenly pinned in the middle of a circle of hot-red beams.

'Intruder alert! Intruder alert! Intruder alert!' shrieked the skulls, their bony jaws creaking like rusty hinges.

'Quick!' said Orpheus's muffled voice from inside the bottle. 'Show them the ring!'

Demon got his hand out from underneath him and waved Hades' black ring at them. As soon as it touched one of the red beams, they all winked out. 'False alarm! Stand down, boys!' said the nearest skull. Demon looked around nervously. Had Hades heard them? He hoped not.

He jumped to his feet, wincing at the pain of his scraped toes, then remembering that they'd be much much sorer if Hades decided to tie him to a big fiery wheel and toast them. How much time did he have left before the Lord of the Underworld came after him? He *had* to find that cauldron quickly.

Offy and Yukus were just slithering down his legs

and starting to mend his feet when he noticed all three of Cerberus's noses twitch.

'Oh no,' he said to the box. 'I think he's going to . . .'

A-AA-A-A-AA-A-CCCCHHHHHOOOOOOO!! A-AA-A-A-AA-A-CCCCHHHHHOOOOOOO!! A-AA-A-A-AA-A-CCCCHHHHHOOOOOOO!! AAAAARRROOOOO!

A-AA-A-A-AA-A-CCCCHHHHHOOOOOOO!! A-AA-A-A-AA-A-CCCCHHHHHOOOOOOO!! A-AA-A-A-AA-A-CCCCHHHHHOOOOOOO!! AAAAARRROOOOO

A-AA-A-A-AA-A-CCCCHHHHHOOOOOOO!! A-AA-A-A-AA-A-CCCCHHHHHOOOOOOO!! A-AA-A-A-AA-A-CCCCHHHHHOOOOOOO!! AAAAARRROOOOO

The hell-hound's three heads crashed to the ground, making everything shake and shudder. A deep new crack snaked out underneath them, and out of it came a roar. Demon recognised that roar. It was the sound of a thousand hungry hundred-armed monsters.

'Box!' shouted Demon. 'Do something! Please!'

The silver lid flew open and the disc on a bendy metal tube shot out, attaching itself to Cerberus's heaving chest then retracting into the box like a whip. The box snapped shut.

'Sneezing symptoms should not have resumed for one hour four minutes and forty-five seconds. Running emergency diagnostics,' it shrieked.

Demon clenched his fists, trying not to panic. The multicoloured snakes that made up Cerberus's manes were beginning to sway and stir. Then the box's lid lifted again. A large brass tube, with something that looked like a thin pointy quill on one end and a ring on the other, popped up from its depths.

'Inject patient's heart with contents of syringe,' squawked the box. 'Hurry!'

Demon didn't understand.

'What do you MEAN?' he screamed.

'Stick him with the pointy end and push!' Its metallic voice rose to a screech.

So Demon grabbed the brass tube and ran over to Cerberus, feeling desperately for his heartbeat again, as he saw the six nostrils twitch again ominously. Where WAS it? His fingers scrabbled over the huge chest, and then down into the left armpit.

*Thuddity-thud. Thuddity-thud.* There it was. He jabbed the pointy end up into the beast-dog's ribs and pushed down on the ring, which slid down into the tube with a hiss. Cerberus's body jerked once and then lay still again. The mane-snakes subsided, and Demon sat back on his heels, listening nervously to the furious bellowing coming out of the crack to his left. Would the hundred-armed monsters be able to get out? He didn't want to be around if they did!

'Emergency averted,' said the box smugly. 'You have one hour precisely to complete your task.' The blue symbols inside flashed twice, and then the lid shut with a bang. 'Battery recharge pending. Shutdown imminent.' It sighed deeply, made a strange pinging sound and went totally silent.

'Nooooo!' Demon yelled, shaking it by both handles and rattling the lid. 'You can't go to sleep NOW!'

But the box stayed a lifeless silver lump. Nothing Demon said or did would move it or wake it up. Finally, almost speechless with terror and frustration, he remembered to let Orpheus out of his bottle.

'What am I going to DO?' he asked, as the mist flowed out and re-formed into his ghostly friend. The box had been his saviour so often that he didn't know how he was going to manage without its tinny advice.

'Steal the cauldron, get back here quick, and hope it recovers in time,' said Orpheus. 'Didn't you hear it? We have less than an hour. Come on!' He flowed towards the black stone doors of the palace. Demon ran beside him, ignoring the ever-increasing roars behind him. One touch of Hades' ring on the doors and they opened. They were in!

Edging around the sides of a large courtyard that had a dead weeping willow and a sluggish fountain in the centre, Orpheus put a finger to his lips.

'This way, I think,' he whispered, leading Demon into a wide passageway lined with giant stone skeletons, standing perfectly still and staring silently at each other across the shiny marble flags. Demon looked at them uneasily as he tiptoed past, but they didn't move a fingerbone. The atmosphere was dull and stifled, so quiet that Demon felt as if he was underwater. He really *really* hoped Orpheus knew where he was going.

His thumping heartbeat ticked away the seconds loudly as they ran up narrow black marble staircases and down broad empty corridors, though his bare feet were almost as noiseless as his ghost friend's. Then, just as Demon smelled the scent of newly mown hay – surprising in that fusty musty place – they heard the sound of muffled marching footsteps.

'Quick! Behind here!' Orpheus hissed, disappearing into an alcove behind a black velvet curtain. Demon slipped in with him, feeling the clammy mist of Orpheus's ghostly body touch his side. He peeked out through a tiny crack to see a terrifying sight. A whole platoon of the giant stone skeletons had come to life and were marching in perfect step down the corridor, bones clicking softly as they passed.

'What are THEY?' Demon whispered, though he feared he knew. Immediately, the skeletons stopped dead, skulls turning towards the alcove as one. Demon froze, not daring to move even an eyelash, let alone breathe. Seeing and hearing nothing they marched on, rows and rows of them. Demon let out a whooshing breath as the last of them disappeared.

'Phew!' he said.

'Definitely phew! Those were the Skeleton Guard, Hades' personal protection force,' Orpheus replied. 'The ones Eurydice was talking about. We passed the spares on the way. Didn't you notice?'

'I thought they were just statues,' Demon said. Then he smelled the new-mown hay again. The scent seemed to be coming out of a door just ahead. A door with a silver crown and a stalk of wheat carved into the stone wall above it. 'Hey! Are those Queen Persephone's chambers?' he hissed. She was the goddess of spring and growing things, after all, as well as Hades' wife.

'Yes, they are. Wait there! I'm just going to check there's nobody inside,' said Orpheus. 'Persephone's due to leave for the upper world soon, but I think she's still here.' He flitted across the corridor and poked his head inside the Queen of the Underworld's apartments. Demon jiggled from foot to foot impatiently, but soon Orpheus was beckoning him forward.

'Coast's clear,' he said. 'I think they're usually in the big hall at this time of day, judging the dead.

Either one of the gods is on your side, or you're just very lucky!'

Demon sent a quick thought of thanks to Heffy, Hestia and Hermes, just in case. If any of the gods were going to be on his side, they certainly were.

Queen Persephone's chambers were a riot of colour, festooned with flowers so bright that they almost hurt Demon's eyes after all the grey and black. He suddenly realised how much he missed Olympus and the stables. Were his beasts all right? Was Doris cleaning out the poo properly and feeding everyone? But there was no time to dwell on that. The clock was ticking and they needed to find that cauldron urgently.

Demon and Orpheus moved quickly through the rooms, searching. Eurydice hadn't been able to remember exactly where she'd seen it. 'There were pretty berries near it, I think,' she'd said. 'Red ones, like lots of tiny cherries.'

There wasn't a berry in sight in any of the rooms. Not a single one. Demon was in despair, looking under drifts of poppies and behind clumps of bluebells.

'We'll never find it,' he groaned. Even the normally cheerful Orpheus looked glum.

'It's all spring flowers in here,' he said. 'Maybe my Eurydice got it wrong.'

Suddenly Demon had a brainwave.

'What if Queen Persephone had her autumn decorations up when Eurydice was here?' he asked. 'This definitely looks like spring, but those tiny red berries come in autumn from trees like mountain ash and hawthorn. Maybe we should be looking for the blossom that grows on those trees.'

They searched every tree in the place. There was cherry blossom and apple blossom, pear blossom and plum blossom, but they couldn't find a single hawthorn or mountain ash tree. Demon was about to tear his hair out with frustration when his eye fell on a little shrub with shiny reddish bark and clouds of tiny white flowers, half-hidden behind a high wall covered in ferns. Between its moss-covered roots he saw a glint of gold. Demon ran over and, with a shout of triumph, put his hand in and pulled. Out came a tiny cauldron with a silver handle.

'Got it!' he cried. Just then there was a tremor beneath his feet, and a muffled rumble. 'Oh no! I think Cerberus has started sneezing again! RUN!'

# 9

# THE CAULDRON OF HEALING

Demon and Orpheus ran at top speed back the way they'd come, avoiding more marching Skeleton Guards by the skin of their teeth, and burst out through the black stone doors again.

'Box! Box! Wake up! I've got the Cauldron of Healing!' Demon shouted, just as three enormous sneezes and howls shook the earth again.

Several things happened at that point.

The box woke up with a screech, glowed blue,

shot out its mechanical arm and grabbed the cauldron from Demon and scuttled towards Cerberus.

'Implementing potion interface, implementing potion interface,' it gabbled, vibrating so fast that it had become a silver blur.

Just then, with a burst of foul gas, several scaly green arms, with suckered tentacle fingers on the ends, erupted out of the crack in the ground near Demon's feet, feeling blindly about for prey.

'AARRGGH!' Demon screamed, jumping for cover behind Cerberus's huge body as the tentacle fingers sensed him and made a grab. Orpheus slipped in beside him, a tiny smudge of mist.

'What's happening?' the ghost boy shouted.

But there was no time for Demon to answer. Instead he pointed with a shaking finger at the black doors, which had just crashed open. A whole platoon of Skeleton Guards came pouring out, stone swords raised, and started hacking at the scaly arms and tentacles. Green blood pooled on the dusty ground, smoking and bubbling, and the roars turned to shrieks of agony, as Cerberus sneezed and howled for a third time, and yet more tentacle fingers reached for the edges of yet another newly formed crevasse.

Amid the chaos of what was happening, Demon was trying hard not to panic. He watched the box like a hawk, willing it to hurry. Was it slowing down? Yes! Yes, it was! He scrambled over Cerberus's furry back, getting bitten by six of the mane snakes – now a hissing angry mass – on the way.

'Ow! Ow! Ow!' he howled, batting them off as Offy and Yukus raced from his neck to suck away the poison. The box snapped open, and then the small golden cauldron floated up out of its insides, filled with a liquid which glowed bright purple. A small funnel was now attached to its side.

'Patient must ingest potion immediately, patient must ingest potion immediately,' it beeped loudly. Demon seized the cauldron by its silver handle and started trying to get the purple liquid into each of Cerberus's three jaws in turn. The pairs of doggy lips were slippery and hard to hold open for the funnel, let alone getting it between the teeth, and soon Demon's hands were so slimy with drool that pouring the medicine in was a real challenge.

'C'mon, Cerberus, open wide! And don't sneeze, don't sneeze, don't sneeze, don't sneeze,' he muttered over and over again as he worked faster than he ever had before. As Cerberus slobbered and dribbled and swallowed, the yellow oozy slime miraculously began to disappear from around each of the hound's six nostrils. He opened his eyes, no longer puffy and swollen, and got up and shook himself, making Demon roll hurriedly out of the way of his enormous lion's paws. Three huge heads gazed down at him. Three huge tongues lolled out between hundreds of sharp white teeth, each dripping poisonous beastdog slobber, which burned holes as it hit the ground.

'Thank you, son of Pan,' said three booming dog-voices and a thousand hissing snake ones.

'N-no problem,' said Demon nervously, backing away slightly. That slobber would hurt if it dripped on his bare skin.

Then Cerberus raised his heads and sniffed the air.

'WOOOOFFFF!' he bayed out of all three mouths. 'WOOOFFF! WOOOFFFF! WOOOFF!'

He charged at the silver gate, which flew open as

the huge beast hit it. Demon and Orpheus stared as Cerberus raced towards the plain, booming barks and howls echoing behind him all the way. Suddenly there was a cacophony of human yells and screams, and they watched as Georgios, the annoying tour guide, flung his red placard away and took to his heels, running as fast as he could, stomach wobbling before him. The Guardian of the Underworld soon caught up with him and tossed him from one head to the other over and over again.

'Serves him right,' said Orpheus unsympathetically. 'Humans aren't meant to come to the Underworld while they're still alive. I hope Cerberus eats him.'

'I do ssso agree with you, dear Orpheusss,' said a soft, sibilant voice behind them. 'But it'sss not Georgioss'sss time to die yet. He'll have a few holes in him, but he'll live. My guardian will sssimply play with him for a while, then herd him and hisss cussstomersss back to the upper world.'

Demon whirled round and fell to his knees as Hades dropped a black-gauntleted hand on his shoulder. Queen Persephone stood at his side, dressed in a robe woven from thousands of sweet-smelling spring flowers. As he saw them, Orpheus dissolved into a streak of mist and disappeared through the open gates with a ghostly moan of fear.

'Jussst in time, ssstable boy. Jussst in time. My ghossst dragonsss will be disssapointed. Are you sssure you wouldn't like to give them sssome sssatisssfaction? Or perhapsss you ssshould ssstay down here and be MY ssstable boy? After all, you did ssso nearly fail to cure my guardian in time. Look at how the monsssstersss almossst got out. I think you owe it to me, really.' He turned and walked over towards where Cerberus had lain, kicking at a few stray tentacles.

Demon shuddered at the terrible thought of being stableboy to Hades, and trapped down here forever. 'N-n-n-no th-th-thank you, Y-Y-our I-I-Impressively D-D-Deathly I-I-Illustriousness. It would b-b-be a h-huge honour, b-but I-I-I'll p-pass.' Over Hades' shoulder he could see a few of the Skeleton Guard, their grey stone bones spattered with green blood, still battling the last few monster arms. The rest were busy with stone shovels, filling in the cracks in the ground, and throwing cut-off arms back down where they had come from. It was a gruesome sight.

Hades looked slyly back at Demon. 'Well, if you're really sssure,' he said. 'I ssssupposse my Sssskeleton Guard did enjoy their little bit of sssword-play. They get ssso little fun. But I must inssssissst you come to a little farewell feassst with me and my dear queen, Persssephone. Ssshe's jusssst about to leave me.' He sighed, and even from a distance his breath stank like month-old corpses. 'I'm sssure you're VERY hungry by now! You wouldn't want to make me crossssss again, now would you, ssstable boy? There'sss ssstill that fiery wheel I mentioned.'

'Oh don't be such a grouchy old god, Hades dear,' said Persephone, coming forward and ruffling Demon's hair with a hand that smelled of fragrant orange blossom. 'We're so grateful to you for curing our poor hound, Pandemonius. Do come to dinner. We serve very nice pomegranate pasties. They'll make a change from that revolting ambrosia.' Demon stared at her. He'd thought all the gods and goddesses loved ambrosia. The idea of food – any kind of food – made his mouth fill with sweet saliva, and he willed his stomach not to rumble. He was *starving*, but he knew he mustn't accept the King and Queen of

Death's invitation, not unless he wanted to be trapped in the Underworld forever. What could he say? How could he get out of it? How could he prevent Hades from forcing him to be the Underworld stable boy, or toasting his toes to a frazzle if he refused? And Persephone seemed nice, but would she turn him into a bed of lilies if he didn't come? There was an uncomfortable silence as Demon thought feverishly.

'There'll be ssstuffed vine leavesss and roasssted sssalmon and honey cakesss as well,' Hades added temptingly.

'And a whole bowl of my special lemon and orange sweeties with sour sugar all to yourself. How can you resist those?' Persephone asked, her voice like melting butter.

Demon's mouth watered. Could it really do any harm? Just a bite of honey cake? Just a tiny piece of salmon? Just a morsel of vine leaf? Just one little sweetie? He was about to say yes when an invisible hand clamped over his mouth, making him dumb for the vital second he needed to stop and realise what the consequences of his answer would have been.

'Hello, dear Uncle Hades,' said Hermes, pulling off his invisibility hat and popping into view, giving Demon a stern shake as he did so. 'Nice to see you, Auntie Seph. Must rush though. Zeus wants his Official Beastkeeper back. Preferably in one piece. So kind of you both to invite him to dinner, but he'll have to decline.'

With that, he tossed his hat back onto his head and seized Demon with one invisible hand. Demon gave a start as his body disappeared from sight. The box was whisked away into invisibility too, and with a whoosh they rose into the air and zoomed off, leaving Hades hissing and screaming with frustration and rage behind them.

'Wretched messssssenger,' he howled. 'Jussst wait till I get my handsss on you! I WANTED that ssstable boy!'

'See you soon, Hermy,' cried Persephone, waving. 'Do visit again. Give my love to dear Zeusy.'

'Lucky I was about,' said Hermes. 'Or you might have been in real trouble.'

Demon let out the breath he'd been holding ever since Hermes had picked him up. His heart felt as if it was trying to crawl out from under his ribs. What a narrow escape he'd had! He imagined having to be stable boy to Hades and shivered. It would have been TERRIBLE.

'Thank you, Hermes,' he said, gratefully.

'Hey, think nothing of it,' replied the god, sniggering slightly. 'Anything to annoy old Death-face. He was very annoyed, wasn't he?'

Demon swallowed. 'W-will Hades come after me again?' he asked.

'No, no, don't worry, Pandemonius. Persephone will calm him down. It's me he's really angry with. But I'd avoid him for a bit just the same.'

Demon vowed silently to do just that.

# 10

# RETURN TO OLYMPUS

As they sped away, Demon tried to look down at himself. It was a very odd experience being invisible. He could feel his body perfectly well, and he could feel Hermes holding onto his hand. He just couldn't see anything except the landscape below. He drew his legs up at the sight of the angry ghosts milling about on the banks of the boiling Styx.

'I think we'll give old Charon a miss this time round,' said Hermes. 'I wasn't lying when I said Zeus wants you back quickly. The stables are starting to smell again. Aphrodite is complaining that all her nightdresses stink of poo.'

'Oh no!' Demon exclaimed. 'What happened? I left Doris the Hydra in charge. It was supposed to clean up and feed everyone.'

'Ah!' said Hermes. 'The Hydra, eh? Well, I'm sorry to tell you there's been a little problem.' Demon clutched hard at the invisible hand holding his as they veered and swerved round the corners of the dark tunnels.

'W-what problem?' he asked, beginning to feel a bit queasy even though he was still starving hungry.

'Apparently it, er, snacked on too much ambrosia cake instead of giving it to the other beasts. It's been lying in its pen moaning with a bad stomach-ache ever since you left.'

'Oh! Poor Doris!' said Demon. 'It's not really very clever. Maybe it misunderstood me.' He hated to think of any of his beasts being in pain or discomfort. 'Can Iris take us back really quickly? I need to give it something from the box.'

Quite soon, he wished he hadn't asked that question. Hermes took him at his word, and the super-fast version of the Iris Express was even more scary and sick-making than the normal one. It was all Demon could do to hold on. His whole face felt as if it was being forced backwards as they zoomed upwards at warp speed. He fell out onto the warm, sunbaked earth of Mount Olympus gasping and wheezing. Hermes placed the medical box gently beside him.

'I've got another message to deliver,' the winged god said. 'See you around!' And with that, he was gone again. The familiar and unpleasant smell of beast-poo drifted into Demon's nostrils as he hauled himself upright and wobbled off towards the stables, the box in his arms.

'About time, Pan's scrawny kid,' said Arnie grumpily, from its post beside the Hydra's pen. 'I'm STARVING!'

'*FOOD-FOOD-FOOD-FOOD!*' went a chorus of barks, moos, baas, squeals, squeaks, hisses and neighs.

'ALL RIGHT!' Demon yelled. 'I'll feed you as soon as I've cured Doris!' He looked at the box. 'Come on,' he said. 'A Hydra stomach-ache should be easy after what we've just been through.'

Ten minutes later Doris was sleeping contentedly, little whuffling snores coming out of its nine heads, and Demon was busy shovelling ambrosia cake and golden hay into mangers. Soon there was the sound of happy chomping. His own stomach was grumbling urgently as he went to get his barrow, brush and shovel. Could he risk popping over to Hestia's kitchen to see if there was a spare something he could eat? No, he decided. He didn't want Aphrodite complaining again. The fewer gods and goddesses who wanted to turn him into little piles of ash, the better. Stuffing several piece of ambrosia cake into his mouth at once, he chewed them down thankfully. They didn't taste half bad after a whole day of Underworld adventures.

Demon tipped barrowload after barrowload down the poo chute, but there was a deathly hush from the hundred-armed monsters below. Maybe they were busy regrowing the arms and tentacle fingers the Skeleton Guard had cut off, he thought, feeling a little bit sorry for them – though not too much. He remembered all too well how it felt to have those suckery things groping about, ready to grab him and pull him down to Tartarus. He swept and shovelled till he was totally exhausted, only just avoiding the Giant Scorpion's sting, which made him think of the ghostly Orion down in the Underworld. He wondered how Orpheus was doing too, feeling sad that they hadn't had a chance to say goodbye. When the stables were spick and span again, he put all his tools away and slumped down on a bale of golden hay, feeling Helios's rays warming him through.

'Pleased to be back?' asked Arnie, pecking him affectionately on the shoulder

'SO pleased,' said Demon, with an enormous yawn, snuggling up against its warm yellow body. It was a first. Arnie had never let him do that before. 'Home at last,' he mumbled drowsily, stroking the soft feathery head with one hand as his eyes closed.

'I wouldn't get too comfortable, stable boy,' Arnie whispered in his ear. 'Because another Important Visitor turned up here last night.'

But Demon was fast asleep and didn't hear him.

# GLOSSARY

## BEASTS:

**Basilisk** (*BASS-uh-lisk*): King of the serpents. Every bit of him is pointy, poisonous, or perilous.

**Cerberus** (*SER-ber-us*): Huge three-headed, snake-maned hound, Guardian of the Underworld, and Hades' favourite cuddly pet.

**Chiron** (*KY-ron*): A super-centaur – part horse, part man, with all the best parts of each.

**Cretan Bull** (*KREE-tun*): A furious, fire-breathing bull. Don't stand too close.

**Griffin** (*GRIH-fin*): Couldn't decide if it was better to be a lion or an eagle, so decided to be both.

**Hydra** (*HY-druh*): Nine-headed water monster. Hera somehow finds this loveable.

**Ladon** (*LAY-dun*): A many-headed dragon that never sleeps (maybe the heads take turns?).

**Minotaur** (*MIN-uh-tor*): A monster-man with the head of a bull. Likes eating people.

**Nemean Lion** (*NEE-mee-un*): A giant, indestructible lion. Swords and arrows bounce off his fur.

**Stymphalian Birds** (*stim-FAY-lee-un*): Man-eating birds with metal feathers, metal beaks and toxic dung.

## GODS AND GODDESSES:

**Aphrodite** (*AF-ruh-DY-tee*): Goddess of Love and Beauty and all things pink and fluffy.

**Ares** (*AIR-eez*): God of War. Loves any excuse to pick a fight.

**Athena** (*a-THEE-na*): Goddess of Wisdom and defender of pesky, troublesome Heroes.

**Artemis** (*AR-te-miss*): Goddess of the Hunt. Can't decide if she wants to protect animals or kill them.

**Dionysus** (*DY-uh-NY-suss*): God of Wine. Turns even sensible gods into silly goons.

**Hades** (*HAY-deez*): Zeus's youngest brother and the gloomy Ruler of the Underworld.

**Helios** (*HEE-lee-us*): The bright, shiny and blinding God of the Sun.

**Hephaestus** (*hih-FESS-tuss*): God of Blacksmithing, Metal, Fire, Volcanoes, and everything awesome.

**Hera** (*HEER-a*): Zeus's scary wife. Drives a chariot pulled by screechy peacocks.

**Hestia** (*HESS-tee-ah*): Goddess of the Hearth and Home. Bakes the most heavenly treats.

**Persephone** (*per-SEF-oh-nee*): Goddess of Spring, stolen away by Hades to be his wife. Made bad mistake of eating pomegranate seeds in the Underworld.

**Poseidon** (*puh-SY-dun*): God of the Sea and controller of supernatural events.

**Zeus** (*ZOOSS*): King of the Gods. Fond of smiting people with lightning bolts.

# OTHER MYTHICAL BEINGS:

**Arachne** (*ar-AKK-nee*): Brilliant weaver. Turned into a spider by Athena for boasting about her skill. Oops.

**Cherubs** (*CHAIR-ubs*): Small flying babies. Mostly cute.

**Dryads** (*DRY-ads*): Tree spirits. Only slightly more serious than nymphs.

**Epimetheus** (*ep-ee-MEE-thee-us*): Prometheus's silly brother who designed animals. Thank him for giving us the platypus and naked mole rat.

**Eurydice** (*YOUR-id-ee-see*): Tree-nymph and all-time greatest love of Orpheus. Stepped on a snake by mistake. Died.

**Geryon** (*JAYR-ee-un*): A cattle-loving Giant with a two-headed dog.

**Heracles** (*HAIR-a-kleez*): The half-god 'hero' who was given twelve impossible tasks by scary Hera, including stealing poor Cerberus from the Underworld and dragging him up to Earth. Loooves killing magical beasts.

**Lethe** (*LEE-thee*): Memory-stealing spirit of forgetfulness. Lives in a marsh.

**Naiads** (*NYE-ads*): Water spirits. Keeping Olympus clean and refreshed since 5,000 BC.

**Nymphs** (*NIMFS*): Giggly, girly, dancing nature spirits.

**Orion** (*oh-RY-on*): Starry hunter killed by a scorpion.

**Orpheus** (*or-FEE-us*): Magnificent musician who tried

to rescue his beloved Eurydice from the Underworld. (Massive fail there, then.)

**Pandora** (*pan-DOR-ah*): The first human woman. Accidentally opened a jar full of evil.

**Prometheus** (*pruh-MEE-thee-us*): Gave fire to mankind, and was sentenced to eternal torture by bird-pecking.

**Satyrs** (*SAY-ters*): 50% goat, 50% human. 100% party animal.

**Silenus** (*sy-LEE-nus*): Dionysus's best friend. Old and wise, but not that good at beast-care.

# PLACES:

**Arcadia** (*ar-CAY-dee-a*): Wooded hills in Greece where the nymphs and dryads like to play.

**Tartarus** (*TAR-ta-russ*): A delightful torture dungeon miles below the Underworld.

**The Underworld**: Hades' happy little kingdom of dead people, also known as Hell in Northern parts.